比较文学与世界文学 研究丛书

主编 曹顺庆

二编 第 **28** 册

英文阅读与古诗英译(下)

张 智 中 著

花木兰文化事业有限公司

国家图书馆出版品预行编目资料

英文阅读与古诗英译（下）/张智中 著 -- 初版 -- 新北市：
花木兰文化事业有限公司，2023〔民112〕
目 6+192 面；19×26 公分
（比较文学与世界文学研究丛书 二编 第 28 册）
ISBN 978-626-344-339-6（精装）
1.CST：中国诗 2.CST：翻译
810.8 111022130

ISBN-978-626-344-339-6

比较文学与世界文学研究丛书
二编 第二八册 ISBN：978-626-344-339-6

英文阅读与古诗英译（下）

作 者 张智中
主 编 曹顺庆
企 划 四川大学双一流学科暨比较文学研究基地
总 编 辑 杜洁祥
副总编辑 杨嘉乐
编辑主任 许郁翎
编 辑 张雅淋、潘玟静 美术编辑 陈逸婷
出 版 花木兰文化事业有限公司
发 行 人 高小娟
联络地址 台湾 235 新北市中和区中安街七二号十三楼
电话：02-2923-1455／传真：02-2923-1452
网 址 http://www.huamulan.tw 信箱 service@huamulans.com
印 刷 普罗文化出版广告事业
初 版 2023 年 3 月
定 价 二编 28 册（精装）新台币 76,000 元 版权所有 请勿翻印

英文阅读与古诗英译(下)

张智中 著

目

次

（44）剑门道中遇微雨（陆游）

剑门道中遇微雨　陆游 衣上征尘杂酒痕， 远游无处不消魂。 此身合是诗人未？ 细雨骑驴入剑门。	**Caught in a Drizzle on the Way**　Lu You Weary and travel-worn from the journey, I'm in a terrible state of dirt, my clothes soiled with dust and stains of wine; yet travelling faraway, to any place, is alluring and ravishing. Self-reflection: am I equal to the name of a poet? Riding a donkey, I, drenched in the drizzling rain, enter the Sword Gate Pass, the greatest pass in the world. （张智中　译）

译文中，I'm in a terrible state of dirt，借鉴自英国作家王尔德（Wilde, O.）小说里的句子：

> And had to make his way home through the flues and chimneys, arriving at his own room **in a terrible state of dirt, disorder, and despair**.

> 他不得不从烟道和烟囱逃回自己的房间，身上满是灰尘、狼狈不堪、万念俱灰。

又读英文：

> From your manner and the state of your clothes, I judge that you have made, like me, a good bit of a journey to-day.

> 从你们的外表和衣着，我能断定你们像我一样，今天也赶了很多路了。

再译陆游《剑门道中遇微雨》：

Caught in a Drizzle on the Way　　Lu You

Weary and travel-worn from

　　　a good bit of a journey made

　　　　　today, I am in a bad state of

my clothes, which are soiled

　　　with dust and stains of wine;

　　　　　yet travelling faraway, to any

place, is ravishing. Self-reflection:

　　　am I equal to the name of a poet?

　　　　　Riding a donkey, I, drenched

in the drizzling rain, enter

　　　the Sword Gate Pass, the

　　　　　greatest pass in the world.

（张智中　译）

比较另外两种英译：

Caught Up in a Light Rain on My Way Through Jianmen Pass　Lu You	Caught in a Drizzle at the Jianmen Pass Lu You
My clothes travel-worn with dust and wine stains,	My clothes are travel-stained as well as wine-stained,
No place is unthrilling if you explore wide and far.	Grief grips my heart wherever I journey afar.
Has this body the making of a poet, or no?	Am I one who is fit only to be a writer of poetry,
A fine drizzle sees me riding a donkey into Jianmen Pass.	To enter the Sword Gate in a drizzle riding a donkey?
（任治稷、余正　译）[46]	（文殊、王晋熙、邓炎昌　译）[47]

　　两个英译在语言上虽然也有可取之处，但也有生硬的地方，从而导致译诗语言上的滞涩。比如第一个译文中，形容词 unthrilling，句子 Has this body the making of a poet 等，不太自然顺畅；第二个译文中，第三行，Am I one who is fit only to be a writer of poetry，读来很是别扭。

───────────

46 任治稷、余正，从诗到诗：中国古诗词英译［Z］，北京：外语教学与研究出版社，2006：252。

47 文殊、王晋熙、邓炎昌，唐宋绝句名篇英译［Z］，北京：外语教学与研究出版社，1995：235-236。

（45）琴诗（苏轼）

琴诗 苏轼 若言琴上有琴声， 放在匣中何不鸣？ 若言声在指头上， 何不于君指上听？	**The Lyre** Su Shi Some say music lurks in the lyre; Why then, closed in its case is it dumb? Some say the sound comes from the fingers of the player; Why then on yours do we hear none? （杨宪益 译）[48]

如果我们不考虑杨宪益的名气，平心而言，此译显得平淡。尤其是最后一行：Why then on yours do we hear none? 语言显得不太流畅。在坚持大量阅读英文的情况下，我们尝试给出如下译文：

On the Chinese Lute Su Shi

If we say music is produced from the Chinse lute

itself, why, when it is put back into the box,

there is no more voice? If we say musical

notes are coaxed from between the

fingers of the player, why, with

wonder, cannot we play

a tune just with

our fingers?

（张智中 译）

译诗中，produce, itself, coax, with wonder 等单词或短语的使用，使得译文地道；第二行中，why 与 when, back 与 box 分别押头韵；第三行中，more 与 musical 押头韵；第四行中，notes, coaxed 与 from 等，押元音韵；第五行中，why 与 with 押头韵；第六行中，wonder 与 we 押头韵。因此，虽然译文为自由体，却依然有明显的音韵铿锵。

（46）夜坐有感（范成大）

夜坐有感 范成大 静夜家家闭户眠， 满城风雨骤寒天。 号呼卖卜谁家子？	**Inspired When Sitting Up at Night** Fan Chengda People are all asleep behind closed doors in the still of night When a storm bursts into the town, making it chilly as ice. What family does the man belong to — the fortune-teller

---

48 Yang Xianyi and Gladys Yang. Poetry and Prose of the Tang and Song[Z]. Beijing: Chinese Literature Press, 1984: 244.

| 想欠明朝籴米钱。 | hawking outside?
He must need money to buy tomorrow's rice.
（文殊、王晋熙、邓炎昌　译）[49] |

　　首先，译诗的标题，用 Inspired 来对应"有感"，显然不对：此处"有感"，非灵感。其次，第二行中的 a storm bursts into the town，第三行中的 What family does the man belong to，是不太自然的英文。最后一行，He must need money to buy tomorrow's rice，则是平淡的英文。因此，这样的译文，最多是有点乏味的散文语言。在阅读英文并汲取英文营养的情况下，我们尝试如下英译：

Night Sitting and Hearing　Fan Chengda

A quiet night, the doors of all households closed, people
ready to go to bed; the whole town falls prey to a
riotous storm of winds and rains, and there is
a sudden touch of coldness. A distant lane
is echoing with the hawking of a fortune
teller — he must be in want of
the money to buy rice for the
breakfast of tomorrow.

（张智中　译）

　　译文中，falls prey to，a sudden touch of coldness，be in want of，有英文色彩。因此，译文虽然散体，却有一定的诗意。

（47）夜坐（张耒）

| 夜坐　张耒
庭户无人秋月明，
夜霜欲落气先清。
梧桐真不甘衰谢，
数叶迎风尚有声。 | **Sitting Up at Night**　Zhang Lei
No one is in the courtyard, the autumn moon is bright.
The air is chill before the frost in the night.
The phoenix tree, unwilling to accept its fate,
Rustles its few leaves against the harsh wind.
（文殊、王晋熙、邓炎昌　译）[50] |

49　文殊、王晋熙、邓炎昌，唐宋绝句名篇英译［Z］，北京：外语教学与研究出版社，1995：250。

50　文殊、王晋熙、邓炎昌，唐宋绝句名篇英译［Z］，北京：外语教学与研究出版社，1995：224。

显然，译诗语言基本上是从汉语直接翻译出来，翻译痕迹明显。如 unwilling to accept its fate 和 rustles its few leaves against the harsh wind 等，似乎是"人造语言"，缺少自然与灵性。再看另一个译文：

Sitting in the Night Scene　Zhang Lei

Over the peopleless courtyard the moon shines bright,

Air becomes cool before the fall of frost at night.

To wither Chinese phoenix trees seem unwilling,

Some remaining leaves are still in the wind soughing.

（邢全臣　译）[51]

同样，语言没有任何亮点，而且多滞涩之处。例如第三行，如何理解？"好像不愿意让梧桐树凋谢"？发挥英文优势，运用当代流畅英文，我们试译如下：

A Night View　Zhang Lei

Soulless and voiceless, the courtyard is bathed in the flood

of autumn moon; on the verge of hoar frost descending,

the air is clear and crisp. The parasol tree is standing

straight in the yard, not reconciling itself to the

fading and falling of leaves, a few of which

are still dancing and prattling

in the wind all round.

（张智中　译）

显然，单词头韵和尾韵的使用，增强了诗歌的韵律。最后两行：which are still dancing and prattling in the wind all round，借鉴自下面的英文句子：

The leaves danced and prattled in the wind all round about us.
树叶在我们四周随风飘动，窸窣作响。

（48）池州翠微亭（岳飞）

池州翠微亭　岳飞	Cuiwei Pavilion in Chizhou　Yue Fei
经年尘土满征衣，	In martial attire stained with dust many years old,
特特寻芳上翠微。	I tarry here, taking in the beauty of Cuiwei Hills.
好水好山看不足，	On the sight of our land I feast my eyes greedily

---

51 邢全臣，用英语欣赏国粹：英汉对照［Z］，北京：科学出版社，2008：193。

马蹄催趁月明归。	While the trotting horse urges me to go back by moonlight.（文殊、王晋熙、邓炎昌　译）[52]

只看译诗简短的标题，竟然两个专名：Cuiwei 和 Chizhou，如果我们为读者考虑的话，就不会这么处理了，因为这样的拼音无甚意义。运用流畅英文，我们试译如下：

The Green Pavilion　Yue Fei

Year in year out my army uniform is soiled with

dust; now idle, I come to the Green Pavilion

on horseback in search of flowery scent.

Before my eyes are feasted with fair

hills and fair rills, the clip-clop

brings me homeward in

bright moonlight.

（张智中　译）

（49）题西林壁（苏轼）

题西林壁　苏轼	**Inscription on the Wall of Western Forest Temple**　Su Shi
横看成岭侧成峰， 远近高低各不同。 不识庐山真面目， 只缘身在此山中。	A horizontal view: ridges; a vertical view: peaks; Far and near, high and low, the mountain is all different. The true visage of Mt. Lu is not known in the heart Of the visitors who are in the midst of the mountain. （张智中　译）

后来，读 Thoreau, H. D. 的《寻找精神家园》（*Letters to a Spiritual Seeker*），里面有这样一个句子：

The **aspect** of the world varies from year to year, **as the landscape is differently clothed**, but I find that the truth is still true.

世界的面貌一年不同于一年，如同山水披上不同的衣装，但是我发现真理仍然是真理。

便觉得《题西林壁》可以用这样的句子来译：the landscape is differently

---

52 文殊、王晋熙、邓炎昌，唐宋绝句名篇英译［Z］，北京：外语教学与研究出版社，1995：234。

clothed。

又读到下面三个句子：

His words were followed by **a pregnant pause**.

他讲完话后意味深长地停了一下。

The less I saw of the novel, the better I liked it: **a pregnant reflection**.

我能从小说中读出的东西越少，我对它才越感兴趣，这样的话我还可以有想象的余地。

这里的 pregnant 与 pregnant reflection，可谓耐品耐味。再如下面句子中的 reflection 的运用：

I was at that point **in my reflections**, when I heard my name called.

我正想着这些的时候，忽然听到老师叫我的名字。

Thus the world assumed another and a better **aspect** from the hour that the poet blessed it with his happy eyes.

因此，诗人用快乐的眼光为世界祝福，人间就呈现出另一幅更加美好的模样。

那么，"不识庐山真面目"之"面目"，似可用名词 aspect 来传译。

又一个描写山景的好句子：

Dolph gazed about him, in mute delight and wonder, at these scenes of nature's magnificence. To the left, the Dunderberg reared its woody precipices, **height over height, forest over forest**, away into the deep summer sky.

道尔夫睁大眼睛四处张望，静静地欣赏着这大自然的奇观，品味其中的愉悦和奇妙。在他的左侧，顿德斯堡耸立在树木繁茂的峭壁上，岩壁一层高过一层，树木层层叠叠，直抵高远的夏日天际。

这里，height over height, forest over forest（岩壁一层高过一层，树木层层叠叠），也可用来增译"庐山真面目"，以使译文形象生动。

那么，《题西林壁》改译如下，并比较许渊冲的英译：

The True Aspect of Lushan Mountain Su Shi Viewed horizontally, it is a ridge; vertically, a peak. High and low, far and near, Lushan Mountain varies according as the landscape is differently clothed: a pregnant reflection. Illusory is the true aspect of the mountain, height over height, forest over forest, where we find ourselves. （张智中　译）	**Written on the Wall of West Forest Temple** Su Shi It's a range viewed in face and peaks viewed from the side, Assuming different shapes viewed from far and wide. Of Mountain Lu we cannot make out the true face, For we are lost in the heart of the very place.[53] （许渊冲　译）

许渊冲的英译，与笔者没有借鉴英文之前的英译，在语言上显得平淡。而借鉴英文之后，译文多处出彩。

（50）塞下曲（三）（卢纶）

塞下曲（三）　　卢纶 月黑雁飞高， 单于夜遁逃。 欲将轻骑逐， 大雪满弓刀。	**Border Songs (No. 3)** Lu Lun In moonless night the wild goose flies high, when invaders run away under the cover of night. Cavalrymen are on the verge of pursuing, when their bows and swords are burdened with snow. （张智中　译）

后来，读到这个英文句子：

But, on the instant, **came the sweep and flash of Jonathan's great knife**.

但是，就在那时，乔那森的大刀快速地挥动了一下。

觉得这正是"大雪满弓刀"的英文描写。改译如下：

Border Songs (No. 3) Lu Lun

In moonless night the wild geese fly high,

when invaders flee away in a flurry under

---

53 许渊冲，唐宋诗一百五十首：汉英对照［Z］，北京：北京大学出版社，1995：327。

the cover of night, to be lost in darkness

and distance. Cavalrymen are on

the point of pursuing when,

on the instant, come the

sweep and flash of their

bows & swords, which

are burdened

with heavy

snow.

（张智中　译）

（51）四时田园杂兴（其一）（范成大）

有时，会读到清新可爱的英文表达，出人意表之外。例如：

Harold sat **in a pocket of shade** and briefly watched the copper statue.

哈德罗在一片小阴影中坐了下来，看了一眼铜像。

这里，a pocket of shade 是令人一读而难忘的表达，就用来翻译范成大的绝句：

四时田园杂兴（其一）　范成大 昼出耘田夜绩麻， 村庄儿女各当家。 童孙未解供耕织， 也傍桑阴学种瓜。	**Miscellanies of the Four Seasons (1)**　Fan Chengda In daytime, weeding the field; in nighttime, twisting 　　the twine; village sons and daughters are all 　　engaged. Small children know no tilling 　　or weaving: in a pocket of shade 　　under mulberry trees they 　　are planting melons 　　for fun. （张智中　译）

再来比读许渊冲的英译：

Rural Life　II Summer

Our sons go out to cultivate the fields by day;

By night our daughters weave thread into cloth with ease.

Their children cannot help their parents, so they stay

And learn to sow melon seed 'neath mulberry trees.[54]

显然是两种不同的语言风格了。

（52）送李判官之润州行营（刘长卿）

送李判官之润州行营 刘长卿 万里辞家事鼓鼙， 金陵驿路楚云西。 江春不肯留行客， 草色青青送马蹄。	**Seeing a Friend Off to the Barrack of Runzhou** Liu Changqing Making light of travelling from afar for military service; hills and rills extend along the post route of Runzhou. The riverside spring has no intention to retain the traveler: green grass sees off the horse hooves all along the way. （张智中　译）

读英文：

And his little mare, **as though she knew his thoughts, falls to trotting**.

他那小母马好像明白他的想法，开始小跑起来。

上引诗句："江春不肯留行客，草色青青送马蹄"，尝试散文英译如下：

The lushly green grass, as though she knew the thoughts of riverside spring, is beckoning and seeing off the hooves of the horse who falls to trotting all along the way.

整首诗改译如下：

Seeing a Friend Off to the Barrack of Runzhou　Liu Changqing

Making light of travelling from afar for military

service; hills and rills extend along the post

route of Runzhou. The lushly green grass,

as though she knew the thoughts of

riverside spring, is beckoning and

seeing off the hooves of the

---

54 许渊冲，宋元明清诗选：汉英对照［Z］，北京：海豚出版社，2013：77。

horse who falls to trotting

all along the way.

（张智中　译）

这样一来，译文就形象生动多了。

（53）酬乐天频梦微之（元稹）

酬乐天频梦微之　元稹	**In Reply to Bai Juyi**　Yuan Zhen
山水万重书断绝， 念君怜我梦相闻。 我今因病魂颠倒， 惟梦闲人不梦君。	Hills upon hills and rills after rills, correspondence is broken; solicitous about me, I enter your dream. Now illness renders me mentally crazy: I dream of irrelevant people instead of you. （张智中　译）

读英文：

This trip to Jersey completely absorbed our ideas, was our sole anticipation, **the constant thought of our minds**.

泽西岛之行吸引着我们，成了我们唯一的期待，成了我们不变的梦想。

整首诗改译如下：

In Reply to Bai Juyi　Yuan Zhen

Hills upon hills and rills after rills, broken

is correspondence; when I am the

constant thought of your mind,

I enter your dream. But illness

renders me mentally crazy:

I dream of irrelevant

people, instead

of you.

（张智中　译）

（54）邯郸冬至夜思家（白居易）

读到这样的英文句子：

He **pictured himself returning home**.

他想象自己回到家里。

He moved from end to end of his voluptuous bedroom, **looking again at the scraps of the day's journey that came unbidden into his mind**.

他在自己富丽堂皇的卧室里来回走动着，不由自主地回想起白天旅行时遇到的种种情景。

就想起了白居易的：

邯郸冬至夜思家　白居易

邯郸驿里逢冬至，抱膝灯前影伴身。

想得家中夜深坐，还应说着远行人。

原　译	改　译
Homesick on Winter Solstice in Handan I spend winter solstice at an inn of Handan; clasping my knees, I and my lonely shadow are under the lamp. At my home, family members stay up late, and they must be talking about me, a distant traveler. （张智中　译）	**Homesick on Winter Solstice in Handan** This winter solstice witnesses me at an inn of Handan; clasping my knees, my lonely shadow and I are under the lamp. I picture myself returning home, looking again at the scraps of my family that come unbidden into my mind, I imagine my kinsfolk staying up late into the night, talking about me, a distant traveler. （张智中　译）

译文中，I picture myself returning home 和 looking again at the scraps of my family that come unbidden into my mind，显然是上引英文句子的借用。

然后，又读到一个类似的英文例子：

She couldn't tell what they were saying, but she **imagined the**

content of their exchange and **silently revelled in it**.

　　张玛丽听不清楚他们在说些什么，却在心里编造着那些对话的内容，乐此不疲。

　　这非常接近"想得家中夜深坐，还应说着远行人"的意境。因此，再次改译如下：

Homesick on Winter Solstice in Handan

This winter solstice witnesses me at an inn of Handan;

clasping my knees, my lonely shadow and I are under

the lamp. I picture myself returning home, looking

again at the scraps of my family that come

unbidden into my mind, I imagine my

kinsfolk staying up late into the night,

and imagine the content of their

chatty talk and silently revel

in it, me as the subject,

a distant traveler.

（张智中　译）

比较 Rewi Alley 的译文：

Thinking of Home During the Winter Festival at Handan

I stayed at Handan guest house all

through the Winter Festival, sitting,

clasping my knees, only my shadow to

accompany me, fancying that

my whole family was sitting

in the lamplight talking about a

lonely man on a distant journey.

（Rewi Alley 译）

　　西方译者如 Rewi Alley 等，往往具有英文的语言优势。但是，我们阅读英文之后给出的译文，却不比他的译文差多少。

（55）问刘十九（白居易）

问刘十九　白居易	**Inviting a Friend for a Drink**　Bai Juyi
绿蚁新醅酒， 红泥小火炉。 晚来天欲雪， 能饮一杯无？	A newly brewed wine of Green Ants, a small stove of red clay. Gathering dusk threatens snow: would you, would you come over for a drink? （张智中　译）

后来，读到下面的英文句子：

The room **gets progressively darker** as the rainstorm that is moving across the prairie approaches.

暴雨穿过草原，正在逼近，屋里也越来越暗了。

A bright fire is blazing in the stove, surrounded with boys struggling to get near it to warm themselves.

炉子里的火生得正旺，大家都围着火炉，使劲地挤上前去烤火。

Darcy politely asked them to come inside the house for some tea.

达西客气地邀请他们到屋里喝杯茶。

It must be **a sign of** rain.

一定是快要下雨了。

If there is a hurricane you always see **the signs of it** in the sky for days ahead, if you are at sea.

如果起飓风，几天之前海上就能见到兆头。

The researchers observed the women for **sign**s of the mental condition called depression.

以及霍克斯英译《红楼梦》第八回中的几个句子：

一面命小丫头："来，让你奶奶去也吃一杯搪搪寒气。"

She turned to one of the maids: "Come on' now! **Pour Nannie a**

nice warm cup of wine to keep the cold out!"

难道就不知道酒性最热，要热吃下去，发散的就快。

Wine has an exceptionally fiery nature, and therefore must be drunk warm in order to be quickly digested.

因命："再烫些酒来。姨妈陪你吃两杯，可就吃饭罢。"

She told a maid to heat some more wine. "There! Auntie will **drink a cup or two with you**, and then we shall have some supper."

借鉴上引英文，《问刘十九》改译如下，首先散文体：

A newly brewed wine of Green Ants over a small stove of red clay, in which a bright fire is blazing. As it gets progressively darker, there is a sign of snow in the gathering of darkness: would you care to come inside the house and surround the stove to warm yourself? I will pour you a nice warm cup of wine which is heated, to keep the cold out, since it has an exceptionally fiery nature.

诗体排列如下：

Inviting a Friend for a Drink   Bai Juyi

A newly brewed wine of Green Ants over a small

stove of red clay, in which a bright fire is blazing.

As it gets progressively darker, there is a sign

of snow in the gathering of darkness: would

you care to come inside the house and

surround the stove to warm yourself?

I will pour you a nice warm cup of

wine which is heated, to keep

the cold out, since it has an

exceptionally fiery

nature.

（张智中　译）

虽然文字添加了一些，但诗意也随之增进。

（56）杂诗（三）（无名氏）

杂诗（三）　　无名氏 两心不语暗知情， 灯下裁缝月下行。 行到阶前知未睡， 夜深闻放剪刀声。	**A Miscellaneous Poem (No. 3)**　　Anonymous Two hearts are knowingly affectionate to each other: one is sewing under the lamp and the other is walking under the moon. When he walks to the doorsill he knows she is still busy: the depth of night hears the sound of putting scissors down. （张智中　译）

英文句子：

Some days they did not speak; at other times they chatted; but **they understood each other perfectly without the aid of words, having similar tastes and feelings**.

他们有时不说话，有时聊上几句；趣味相同，感觉相似，无需借助言语，他们相互理解。

这，不正是"两心不语暗知情"吗？

另有英文句子：

They **are busying themselves in** packing up.

他们正忙着整理行装。

…as **the hours crept on**, she sank to sleep.

随着时间的流逝，她睡着了。

改译如下：

A Miscellaneous Poem (No. 3)　　Anonymous

They understand each other perfectly without the aid

of words, having similar tastes and feelings: one

is sewing under the lamp and the other is

walking under the moon. Walking to

the doorsill he knows she is still

busying herself in needlework:

the depth of night hears the

sound of scissors putting

down, as the hours

creep on.

（张智中　译）

这样一来，译诗更添了点儿英诗的味道。

（57）苦热题恒寂师禅室（白居易）

苦热题恒寂师禅室　白居易 人人避暑走如狂， 独有禅师不出房。 可是禅房无热到？ 但能心静即身凉。	**To a Zen Master in Sultry Days**　Bai Juyi Preventive of sunstroke, people all go out; only the zen master remains in his room. Is it that the zen room is free from the heat? A calm heart, if any, renders it cool. （张智中　译）

He was **calm and collected**. Though extremely weak, he had no sensation of pain.

他冷静沉着，尽管他极度虚弱，但没有任何痛苦的感觉。

这里，"冷静沉着"的英文表达 calm 和 collected，既传神又押头韵。整首诗改译如下：

To a Zen Master in Sultry Days　Bai Juyi

Preventive of sunstroke, people all

go out of the heat of the room,

when the Zen master, calm and

collected, stays in his own

room. Is it that the Zen

room is free from the

fierce heat? A calm

heart, if any,

renders it

cool.

（张智中　译）

（58）宿新市徐公店（杨万里）

宿新市徐公店　杨万里	A Summer View　Yang Wanli
篱落疏疏一径深， 树头花落未成阴。 儿童急走追黄蝶， 飞入菜花无处寻。	A sparsely spotted hedge sees a path meandering far away; the trees are shedding off a profusion of petals before shade is produced. Young children are running after a yellow butter- fly, which wings its wild way into the depth of flowers, no- where to be found. （张智中　译）

译文中，a yellow butterfly, which wings its wild way into the depth of flowers, 借鉴自英国作家 Daphne du Maurier 的英文名著 Rebecca 中的一个句子：

A yellow butterfly **winged his foolish way before me to the terrace**.

一只黄色的蝴蝶在我面前胡乱扇动翅膀，向平台飞去。

不仅表意很好，而且，which, wings, wild, way, 四个单词有着非常明显的头韵效果。

（59）岳州守岁（一）（张说）

岳州守岁（一）　张说	Sitting Up in Yuezhou at Night to Welcome in the New Year (No. 1)　Zhang Yue
夜风吹醉舞， 庭户对酣歌。 愁逐前年少， 欢迎今岁多。	Night wind blows drunken dancing; courtyard faces endless singing. Chasing the yesteryear, sorrow is lessened; welcoming in the new year, our joys are heightened. （张智中　译）

后来，读到这句英文：

They were quite unsteady when they came out, owing to the effect of the alcohol on their empty stomachs. It was a fine, mild day, and **a gentle breeze fanned their faces**.

因为空肚喝酒，所以出来时，他们都摇摇晃晃的。天气温暖宜人，一阵和风拂面而来。

《岳州守岁（一）》改译如下：

Sitting Up in Yuezhou at Night to Welcome in the New Year

(No. 1)   Zhang Yue

A gentle night breeze is fanning the faces

of drunken dancers, courtyard faces

endless singing. Chasing yester-

year, sorrow is lessened;

welcoming in the new

year, our joys are

heightened.

（张智中　译）

（60）春晓（孟浩然）

原　诗	英　译
春晓 春眠不觉晓， 处处闻啼鸟。 夜来风雨声， 花落知多少。	Spring Dawn Spring slumber unaware of dawn: here & there, birds are twittering. The night witnesses winds & rains: how many blossoms have been broken? （张智中　译）

译完本诗之后，又读到英文：

One winter **morning shortly before daybreak**, ...

There was no ticking from the hall clock, no humming from the fridge, no **birdsong** from the garden.

挂钟不走了，冰箱不响了，花园里的鸟儿也不叫了。

其中的 birdsong（鸟鸣声），甚觉可爱。

At six o'clock in the morning of February 3, 1981, I **awoke with a start to the sounds of** drums, trumpets, ...

这里，awoke with a start to the sounds of，写听见什么声音而突然醒来，英文表述自然而巧妙。如果借鉴而来英译"春眠不觉晓，处处闻啼鸟"，自然大好。

> Maureen **woke to a bright sky full of promise** and a light breeze that played at the leaves.
>
> 莫琳醒来，看见充满希望的晴空，和拂过树叶的微风。

这个句子中，同样动词 woke 与介词 to 搭配。

又，读到霍克斯英译《红楼梦》：

> 梦中之事便忘了一半。
>
> And there he was sitting in his study, **the contents of his dream already half forgotten**.

霍克斯的英文搭配 the contents of his dream，感觉甚好。若用来英译孟浩然《春晓》之梦，则不失深婉之意。整首诗改译如下：

> **Spring Dawn**   Meng Haoran
>
> One spring morning shortly before daybreak,
>
> spring slumber unaware of dawn, when I
>
> awake with a start to the birdsong from
>
> flowery trees: here, there, everywhere ....
>
> The contents of my dream remain
>
> vivid: against winds and rains,
>
> blossoms have been broken,
>
> how many?
>
> （张智中　译）

译文显有进步。然，后来又读英文：

> He is **a bird of leisure**, and seems always at his ease.
>
> 他喜欢安逸，似乎总是悠然自得。
>
> It **utters a peculiarly liquid April sound**.
>
> 四月里，它发出尤其清澈的叫声。
>
> Our long-tailed thrush, or thrasher, **delights in a high branch** of some solitary tree, whence **it will pour out its rich and intricate warble** for an hour together.

我们的长尾画眉，或者叫长尾莺，栖息在一棵孤树的高枝上，可以鸣叫上整整一个小时。声音丰富且复杂。

One afternoon **a very violent storm arose which made the branches of the trees stream out like wildly disheveled hair**.

直到有一天下午，一场猛烈的风暴来临，树枝像凌乱的头发一样，四处漂流。

显然，这些清新可爱的英文句子，都与《春晓》有密切关系。于是，再次改译如下：

Spring Dawn Meng Haoran
One spring morning shortly before daybreak, spring
slumber unaware of dawn, when I awake with a start
to a birdsong —— the birds of leisure delight in
flowery trees high and low, whence they pour
out their rich and intricate warble, a peculiarly
liquid sound. The contents of my dream
remain vivid: last night a very violent
storm arises which makes branches
stream out like wildly disheveled
hair: blossoms have been
broken, how
many?
（张智中　译）

每天坚持英文阅读，竟然又得几个与《春晓》相关的句子：

Already had the bright sun renewed the day everywhere with its fine beams and **the birds sat merrily singing on the blooming branches**.

明媚的晨光带来了新的一天，小鸟在繁茂的枝头唱着动听的歌。

Now **the sun's golden beams began to emerge** when Madame Fiammetta, **awoken by the sweet singing birds sitting merrily on the trees**, rose from her bed.

旭日的光芒普照大地，鸟儿们正在枝头尽情欢唱。菲亚美达被鸟儿的歌声唤醒，便起了床。

The birds' singing is rare music to them, whose sweet notes put them to sleep, which neither art nor medicine can do.

鸟儿的歌声对于他们来说可是难得的乐曲，悦耳的歌声使得他们入睡，这是任何艺术或药物都没发办到的。

They make their way west, **amidst the sweet singing of pretty birds flying round** and the richly abounding meadows of fair herbs and flowers.

他们一路向西缓缓而行，飞来飞去的小鸟唱着甜美的歌儿，草地上长满了鲜花、香草。

这样，《春晓》又可改译：

Spring Dawn　Meng Haoran

One spring morning shortly before daybreak, the sun renews

the day everywhere with its golden beams which begin

to emerge when I, awoken by the sweet singing birds

flying round or sitting merrily on the blooming

branches, rise from my bed. The birds' singing

is rare music to me, which reminds me of

the contents of my dream: last night

a very violent storm arises which

makes branches stream out

like wildly disheveled

hair: blossoms have

been broken,

how many?

（张智中　译）

这样一来，译文更加繁杂丰富，但却不失英文之味道。关于孟浩然之《春晓》，笔者另有一译：

Spring Dawn　Meng Haoran

I wake to the sound

of a spring dawn, which

is full of a new creation:

the birds are cheeping

and chirping sharply

and crisply, here

and there, not caring

how many blossoms

have been broken by

the nightlong winds

and rains.

（张智中　译）

首行的英译，是读到下面两个英文句子得到的启发：

I woke to the sound of a heavy downpour.

大雨倾盆之声，把我从睡梦中惊醒。

The morning was **full of a new creation**.

早晨，万象更新。

关于副词 sharply，郑易里主编的《英华大词典》中，对其形容词 sharp 有如此解释："［语音］清音的；气音的。"*Collins Cobuild Essential English Dictionary* 的解释：A sharp sound is very short and sudden and quite loud。其他词典里的例子：… the sharp crack of a twig（枝条的折断声）。牛津词典的解释：sharp: shrill; piercing。

另有英文句子用到 sharply，正好是描写鸟叫之声：

The atmosphere was grey and translucent, **the birds sang sharply on the young twigs**, the earth would be quickening and hastening in growth.

天色空濛，鸟儿在新枝上鸣啭，大地上万物竞相勃发。

用词精准之外，here and there 分置两行，以及倒数第二行中的 nightlong 等，都给译诗注入活力。

后来，读到一个英文句子，便再次引发英译《春晓》的欲望：

In a bright sunny morning in early summer, **it was delectable to hear their cheerful notes, as they sported about in the pure, sweet air, chirping forth, as it were, the greatness and prosperity of** the Webbers.

在一个阳关明媚的初夏的早晨，听到鸟儿欢快的叫声是愉悦的。

它们在纯净、甜美的空气中飞舞嬉戏，叽叽喳喳地叫着，仿佛是在说韦伯家族的卓越和兴旺。

这样的英文太好，所描写的鸟，跟孟浩然的春晓之鸟，似曾相识，心灵默契。似可如此借用：

The birds sport about in the pure, sweet air, chirping forth, as it were, the sheer ferocity of last night. （鸟儿在纯净、甜美的空气中飞舞嬉戏，叽叽喳喳地叫着，仿佛是在诉说昨晚的狂风暴雨。）又读到一个短小的英文句子：

A bird is known by its **note**, and a man by his talk.

闻声知鸣鸟，闻言见人心。

可知，鸟啼之声，可用 note(s) 来表示。《春晓》整首诗英译并回译如下：

Spring Daybreak　　Meng Haoran	**春之破晓**　　孟浩然
I wake to the noise of a	春：破晓之声，把
spring daybreak: the birds	我吵醒。鸟儿们在
sport about in the pure,	纯净甜美的空中喊
sweet air, chirping forth,	喊喳喳喊喊喳喳喊
as it were, the sheer ferocity	喊喳喳似乎——昨
of last night. It is lamentable	夜的暴行，回忆中
to hear their notes which,	令人心恸。鸟啼声
here and there, are sharp	声：此起，彼伏；
and crisp. How many	清脆，尖锐。多少
blossoms have been broken	多少花儿——夭折
by the nightlong winds	那整夜的风，那整
& rains? How — many?	夜的雨——多少？
（张智中　译）	（张智中　译）

大概因为《春晓》所绘之景乃常见之景，读英文便也常见类似句子：

A rainy night had been followed by a glorious morning, and the heath-covered country-side with the glowing clumps of flowering gorse seemed all the more beautiful to eyes which were weary of the duns and drabs and slate greys of London.

雨夜过后的清晨阳光灿烂，乡下长满石南灌木丛，点缀着一簇簇盛开的荆豆花，在厌倦阴沉土灰、单调乏味的伦敦的人眼中，这一切显得格外美丽。

Holmes and I walked along the broad, sandy road **inhaling the fresh morning air, and rejoicing in the music of the birds and the fresh breath of the spring**.

福尔摩斯和我漫步在宽阔的沙子路上，呼吸着清晨的新鲜空气，陶醉在春日的鸟语花香之中。

Holmes pointed down the long tract of road which wound, a reddish yellow band, between the brown of the heath and **the budding green of the woods**.

福尔摩斯指着一段长长的路，那条路宛如一条红黄色的带子，镶嵌在那棕褐色的石南灌木丛和一片嫩绿的树林之间。

借用如上英文表达，采取当代英诗常见之建行形式，又得一《春晓》英译：

Glorious Spring Morning　Meng Haoran

A night, a rainy spring night,
　　is followed by a glorious
　　　　morning, into which I am
wakened, to inhale the fresh
　　morning air, to rejoice in the
　　　　overflowing music of the birds
and the fresh breath of the
　　early spring　—　a new creation
　　　　from the nightlong winds and
rains. How many blossoms,
　　from the budding green of
　　　　the woods, have been broken?

（张智中　译）

译者在不同时刻，读一首诗有不同的理解或感悟，便会产生不同的译文，这也是译者主体性的一种体现。因此，诗歌的译者，当为诗人，原因也在于此。译者若非诗人，便不会产生如此丰富而有诗意的联想。那么，他的译诗，就是干瘪的，缺乏情感的。唯有诗人译者，在其诗情被调动起来的时候，就会激发灵感，产生妙译。比读许渊冲的英译：

Spring Morning　Meng Haoran

This spring morning in bed I'm lying,

Not to awake till birds are crying.

After one night of wind and showers,

How many are the fallen flowers!⁵⁵

感觉译文只是浅层之译，未能深入诗理诗情。再看翁显良的散体英译：

One Morning in Spring　Meng Han-ran

Late! This spring morning as I awake I know. All round me the birds

are crying, crying. The storm last night, I sensed its fury. How many, I

wonder, are fallen, poor dear flowers!⁵⁶

译文可谓深情悲叹，入神入化。然而，相较而言，感觉译文还是没有放开，译者的才情，似乎还是受到了束缚。

（61）夜雪（白居易）

原　诗	原　译	改　译
夜雪 已讶衾枕冷， 复见窗户明。 夜深知雪重， 时闻折竹声。	**Night Snow** The quilt is surprisingly cold, and I see my window bright. Deep night knows the heavy snow: occasionally audible is the cracking of bamboo branches. （张智中　译）	**Night Snow** The quilt is unbearably cold, and I see my window bright in the depth of the night. There must be a heavy snow: audible once in a great while is the cracking and crashing of loaded bamboo branches falling far off in woods. （张智中　译）

改译中，the cracking and crashing of loaded bamboo branches falling far off in woods，是下面两个英文句子的改写：

A cracking of branches sent him scurrying forward; only to look back, with his heart wildly beating, and discover a pigeon regaining its balance in a tree.

55　许渊冲，唐诗三百首：汉英对照［Z］，北京：海豚出版社，2013：31。
56　翁显良，古诗英译［Z］，北京：北京出版社，1985：14-15。

突然听到一阵碎裂的响声，他一惊，紧走几步回头一看，才发现是树上一只差点失去平衡的白鸽，他心脏犹兀自急促地跳个不停。

The crash of a loaded branch falling far off in the woods reverberated like a musket-shot.

远处林子里被雪压断的树枝落地，象鸟枪一样轰鸣。

另外，采用 unbearably cold 和 in the depth of the night 等，也是地道的英文表达。于是，改译读来更像一首英诗。

（62）游园不值（叶绍翁）

读到下面英文句子：

Yet now that he was out, and on his feet, it was as if everywhere he looked, **the fields, gardens, trees and hedgerows had exploded with growth.**

但如今站在这里，他无论看向哪儿，那草地、那花园、那树、那篱笆，都散发着藏不住的生机。

Trees and flowers seemed **to explode with colour and scent**.

树和花都争先恐后爆发出各种颜色和香气。

描写花草生长之茂，用动词 explode，何其形象生动！

There came **a tap at her door**.

有人敲门。

As he was speaking there was **a soft tapping at the door**.

就在他说话的时候，突然响起了轻轻的敲门声。

All his **rapping and knocking**, while making loud exclamations, were as **fruitless** as before.

他又是拍门，又是叫喊，不过就跟刚才一样毫无结果。

写扣门而不开，正是"小扣柴扉久不开"了。

... for love, I crept to the edge of a roof to reach \ **a petal-decked branch**.（我，为了爱，爬到屋顶的边缘去够 \ 缀满花瓣的树枝。）

英文造词 petal-decked（花瓣装饰的），何其清新可爱！想起宋人叶绍翁的《游园不值》及早年的英译：

游园不值	**Failing to Meet a Friend**
应怜屐齿印苍苔， 小扣柴扉久不开。 春色满园关不住， 一枝红杏出墙来。	Afraid of my clogs crushing the green sward? The wicket gate refuses to open in spite of my repeated soft tapping. A gardenful of spring is a gardenful of desire: a sprig of apricot flowers is swaying and flaming over the wall. （张智中　译）

如此英译，本已满意。但是，上引之英文句子或词汇实在可爱，且吻合《游园不值》之语境。于是改译如下：

Failing to Meet a Friend　Ye Shaoweng

Afraid of my clogs crushing the green sward?

The wicket gate refuses to open in spite of

my persistent soft rapping, tapping, and

knocking: all fruitless. The garden

is exploding with growth, with

color and scent: a gardenful

of spring is a gardenful

of desire — a petal-

decked apricot branch

is swaying and

flaming over

the wall.

（张智中　译）

如此排列，自是一体。当代诗歌，无论英诗还是汉诗，都有着诗行排列的极大自由。而且，诗人或译者往往因诗制宜，灵感之下，而产生一时一诗的独特的诗行排列。在保持如上译文几乎不变的情况下，笔者另有两种不同的诗歌建行：

Failing to Meet a Friend Ye Shaoweng Afraid of my clogs crushing	**Failing to Meet a Friend**　Ye Shaoweng Afraid of my clogs crushing the green sward? The wicket

the green sward? The wicket 　　gate refuses to open in spite of my persistent rapping, 　　tapping, and knocking…. 　　The garden is exploding with growth, with color 　　and scent: a gardenful of 　　spring is a gardenful of desire　—　a petal-decked 　　apricot branch, over the wall, 　　　is swaying and flaming…. （张智中　译）	gate refuses to open in spite of my persistent rapping, 　　　　　tapping, 　　　　　　knocking…. The garden is exploding with growth, with color and scent: a gardenful of spring is a gardenful of desire　—　a petal-decked apricot branch, over the wall, 　　　　is swaying 　　　　　and flaming…. （张智中　译）

尤其第二种，两个诗节的最后两行，明显往右缩进，暗示着"红杏出墙"之状貌。

又读英文：

A knock at the door brought a quick exclamation from him.

一阵敲门声又引得他立刻大叫起来。

想起"小扣柴扉久不开"，似可英译：

Repeated knockings at the wooden door bring nothing but an empty
　　echo in the yard.

《游园不值》整首诗另译如下：

Failing to Meet a Friend　Ye Shaoweng

Afraid of my clogs crushing
　　　　the green sward? Repeated
　　　　　　knockings at the wooden door
bring nothing but an empty
　　　　echo in the yard ….
　　　　　　The garden is exploding
with growth, with color,
　　　　with scent: a gardenful
　　　　　　of spring is a gardenful
of desire —

> a petal-decked
>
> > apricot branch,
>
> over the wall,
>
> > is swaying
>
> > > and flaming....

（张智中　译）

语言上的借用之外，诗行的排列，再度创新。译诗终于值得回味，成为一首地道的英诗。比较许渊冲和邢全臣的译文：

Calling on a Friend Without Meeting Him　Ye Shaoweng

How could the green moss like my sabots, whose teeth sting?

I tap long at the door, but none opens at my call.

The garden can't confine the full beauty of spring;

An apricot extends a blooming branch o'er the wall.

（许渊冲　译）[57]

An Unsuccessful Visit to the Small Garden　Ye Shaoweng

The host fears that on the moss my clogs will leave footprints,

Long after my light knock he still does not open the wooden gate at all.

The courtyard cannot shut in all the springtime tints,

An apricot branch laden with blossoms has risen above the wall.

（邢全臣　译）[58]

比读之下，语言的醇厚与单薄，显而易见了。

（63）独坐敬亭山（李白）

有时，读到一个英文句子，竟有两个语言亮点可资借用：

I find I **never weary** of great churches. It is **my favourite kind of mountain scenery**.

我发现我对大教堂百看不厌。这是我喜欢的山景。

这里，never weary of 和 my favourite kind of mountain scenery，恰好用来英译李白之诗：

---

57 许渊冲，宋元明清诗选：汉英对照［Z］，北京：海豚出版社，2013：85。

58 邢全臣，用英语欣赏国粹：英汉对照［Z］，北京：科学出版社，2008：227。

独坐敬亭山　李白 众鸟高飞尽， 孤云独去闲。 相看两不厌， 只有敬亭山。	**Sitting Alone in Jingting Mountain**　Li Bai A bevy of birds are all gone; the lonely cloud is wafting alone. We are not tired of each other: Jingting Mountain and I. （张智中　译）

运用上引英文，改译如下，并比较翟理斯（Herbert A. Giles）的英译：

Sitting Alone in Jingting Mountain A bevy of birds are gone, one and all; the lonely cloud is wafting alone, at ease. I never weary of Jingting Mountain, which is my favorite kind of scenery, and the mountain, never weary of me. （张智中　译）	**Companions** The birds have all flown to their roost in the tree, 　The last cloud has just floated lazily by; But we never tire of each other, not we, 　As we sit there together, — the mountain and I. （Herbert A. Giles 译）59

显然，Giles 直译成分较多，汉语痕迹明显。

（64）竹里馆（王维）

竹里馆　王维 独坐幽篁里， 弹琴复长啸。 深林人不知， 明月来相照。	**A Retreat in Bamboos**　Wang Wei Sitting alone in secluded bamboos, I'm whistling and playing the lute. The woods is deep and privy to none: the bright moon is my boon companion. （张智中　译）

后来，偶然读到一首当代英语诗歌及其汉译：

---

59 华满元、华先发，汉诗英译名篇选读 [C]，武汉：武汉大学出版社，2014：205。

The Ponga Grove　Margaret T. South (Australia)	蕨树林　邵梅嘉（澳大利亚）
Alone I sit in a grove of shady pongas I play my transistor and beat time with my pencil In the depths of the Dell no one knows I am there A large weka comes and climbs on my book.	我独坐在蕨树林荫下， 把玩着收音机， 用铅笔敲打着拍子。 没人知道我在这幽深的山谷里， 有一只大昆虫来与我作伴。 还爬到了我的书上。[60]

显然，这首诗与王维《竹里馆》有神似之处。而英诗的一些表达，正可以借用。如 Alone I sit in a grove of，I play my … and …，in the depths of … no one knows I am there 等。

因此，改译如下：

A Retreat in Bamboos　Wang Wei

Alone I sit in a secluded

　　grove of shady bamboos:

I play my lute while whistling

　　along. In the depths of woods

no one knows I am here,

　　and I am privy to none

but the bright moon, who

　　is my boon companion.

（张智中　译）

（65）江雪（柳宗元）

江雪　柳宗元	River Snow　Liu Zongyuan
千山鸟飞绝， 万径人踪灭。 孤舟蓑笠翁， 独钓寒江雪。	Hundreds of hills see no flight of birds; thousands of paths witness no human trace. A lonely boat carries an old man wearing a straw rain hat, who is solitarily angling cold river snow. （张智中　译）

60 刘文杰，英语诗歌汉译与赏析［M］，广州：中山大学出版社，2014：36。

后来，读到同一本书里的另一首英诗及其汉译：

The Fisherman Margaret T. South (Australia) Beside the pool a white haired old man, Quietly he sits, no thought of time. I stop to ask him: "How many fish?" But then I see his rod has no line.	渔翁　邵梅嘉（澳大利亚） 银发老汉，垂钓池畔。 凝神静坐，忘了时间。 驻足请问："钓得几条？" 但见竿头，无丝无钩。[61]

这里的"渔翁"，似乎正是柳宗元的"蓑笠翁"，当然，多有可资借鉴之处。包括《江雪》的标题，如果借用英诗标题 *The Fisherman*，似乎更好。柳宗元《江雪》改译如下：

The Fisherman   Liu Zongyuan

Hundreds of hills cut off flight of birds;

thousands of paths see no human trace.

A lonely boat carries an old fisher-

man wearing a straw rain hat:

quietly he sits, no thought

of time, solitarily

angling cold

river snow.

（张智中　译）

（66）春日偶成（程颢）

有时，读到一个英文句子，也会引起一首诗的改译。比如读到这个句子：

　　Although he was incapacitated, the old man's **heart remained as lucid as a mirror**.

老人不能动，可心像镜子一样明亮。

"像镜子一样明亮"，这样的比喻并非新鲜，而英文 remain as lucid as a mirror，用词鲜活可爱，值得学习借鉴。宋代诗人程颢的诗及其英译：

春日偶成　程颢 云淡风轻近午天， 傍花随柳过前川。	**An Impromptu Poem on a Spring Day** Cheng Hao Pale clouds and a light breeze approach the noon; under willows and beside flowers I stroll along

---

61 刘文杰，英语诗歌汉译与赏析［M］，广州：中山大学出版社，2014：191。

时人不识余心乐， 将谓偷闲学少年。	the river bank. Worldly people know not the joy of my heart: they say I snatch a little leisure from the rush of business, acting like a naughty boy. （张智中　译）

借鉴上引英文句子，改译如下：

An Impromptu Poem on a Spring Day　Cheng Hao

Pale clouds and a light breeze approach the noon;

under willows and beside flowers I stroll along

the river bank. Worldly people know not

the joy of my heart, which remains as

lucid as a mirror — they say I

snatch a little leisure from

the rush of business,

acting like a

naughty

boy.

（张智中　译）

其实，主要添加了 which remains as lucid as a mirror，来修饰"余心"。动词 remain，表示保持童心之意，比 is 要好很多；lucid 则有"清晰的；神智清醒的"之意，比之 bright 或 clear，更加契合这里的语境。于是，译文更加精进。

（67）夜雨寄北（李商隐）

夜雨寄北　李商隐 君问归期未有期， 巴山夜雨涨秋池。 何当共剪西窗烛， 却话巴山夜雨时。	**Northward Missing in a Raining Night**　Li Shangyin You ask the date of my return, which I cannot tell; autumn pool is swollen with night rain in Ba Mountain. When can we together trim candle wicks against the west window and recall the rainy night in Ba Mountain? （张智中　译）

后来，读到 William Maxwell 于 1997 出版的散文集 *So Long, See You Tomorrow*，见到这样一句英文：

At night we undressed and got into bed and fell asleep without taking advantage of the dark **to unburden our hearts to each other**.

这里的搭配，unburden our hearts to each other 非常好，表示互相倾心交谈，正可用来描写"却话巴山夜雨时"的状貌。于是，《夜雨寄北》改译如下：

Northward Missing in a Raining Night　Li Shangyin

You ask the date of my return, about which

I am not sure; autumn pool is swollen

with night rain in Ba Mountain.

When can we get together to

trim candle wicks against

the west window and

recall the rainy night

in Ba Mountain,

unburdening our

hearts to each

other?

（张智中　译）

又，读英国作家史蒂文森（Stevenson, R. L.）的《内河航行记》，见到这样两个英文句子：

The river **was swollen with the long rains**.

接连不断的雨水使河水涨了起来。

Such a dinner as we were going to eat! such beds as we were to sleep in! — and all the while the rain raining on houseless folk over all the poplared countryside!

想象一下我们一会儿会吃到怎样的美味，睡怎样舒适的床！——旅居他乡的游子在白杨瑟瑟的乡村整夜听雨！

原译中，is swollen with night rain，根据第一个句子，似可改成 is swollen with the long night rains；而第二个英文句子中，the rain raining 的搭配，令人感到新鲜。用 rain 的动词形式，来搭配其名词，如果不是读到这样的英文原著，我们肯定不会这样用，甚至还会怀疑这句子不符合英文习惯或语法了。再做细想，便觉这样搭配深有余味了。那么，便可考虑在刚才的改译 is swollen with the long night rains 再加上一个定语从句，成为：is swollen with the long night rains which are raining endlessly。整首诗改译如下：

Northward Longing in a Rainy Night　　Li Shangyin
You ask the date of my return, about which I am
not sure; autumn pool, in Ba Mountain, is swollen
with the long night rains which are raining
endlessly. When can we get together to
trim candle wicks against the west
window and recall the rainy night
in Ba Mountain, unburdening
our hearts to each
other?
（张智中　译）

另外，还有几处改译。标题中，Missing 改成 Longing，Raining 改成 Rainy，似更贴切。原译中的最后四行，其实是一个英文句子：When can we together trim candle wicks against the west window and recall the rainy night in Ba Mountain? 改译：When can we get together to trim candle wicks against the west window and recall the rainy night in Ba Mountain, unburdening our hearts to each other? 把 together 改成 get together to，语气更加流畅自然。

（68）题兴化寺园亭（贾岛）

题兴化寺园亭　贾岛 破却千家作一池， 不栽桃李种蔷薇。 蔷薇花落秋风起， 荆棘满亭君自知。	**Inscription on a Pavilion in Xinghua Temple**　　Jia Dao A thousand households have been leveled to build a garden, where roses are planted instead of peaches and plums. When autumn wind blows flowers aground, the pavilion is covered with briers & brambles, which sting. （张智中　译）

读英文：

> His house should be situated near a source of water, surrounded by a garden with **bowers**, and divided into different compartments for different purposes.

这里的 bower，意为"树荫处（凉亭）；闺房。"

又读到英文书 *The Uses of Sadness* 中的一个短语：

> ... a hotel lobby, a leafy garden **arbour**.

这里的 arbour，是"藤架；凉亭"之意。

于是，觉得原译中的 pavilion（亭子；楼阁），似可改成 arbour（藤架；凉亭）。

《题兴化寺园亭》改译如下：

Inscription on an Arbour in Xinghua Temple   Jia Dao

A thousand households have been

leveled to build a garden, where

roses are planted instead of

peaches and plums. When

autumn wind blows

flowers aground,

a thorny arbour

reveals itself

before you.

（张智中　译）

后来，又读到一个英文句子：

> It was early summer, not yet unbearably hot. The clematis vine was in full bloom, and blackberries trailed along the fence **in wild profusion**.

如果说 in profusion 可用来描写花卉植物生长茂盛，in wild profusion 则是描写植物长疯了：描写花卉植物的疯长状貌，恰到好处。那么，"荆棘满亭君自知"，若用 in wild profusion，该是得来全不费工夫了。《题兴化寺园亭》再次改译如下：

Inscription on an Arbour in Xinghua Temple   Jia Dao

A thousand households have been

leveled to build a garden, where

roses are planted instead of

peaches and plums. When

autumn wind blows

flowers aground,

an arbour is thorny

with undergrowth

in wild profusion.

（张智中　译）

（69）小雪（清江）

小雪　清江 落雪临风不厌看， 更多还恐蔽林峦。 愁人正在书窗下， 一片飞来一片寒。	**Light Snow**　Qing Jiang Snowflakes dancing in the wind: a sightly sight; all of them vanish into forests and mountains. A doleful man is standing at the study window: a flake of flying snow is a flake of coldness. （张智中　译）

读英文：

And he sat looking at the snow, which **was coming down in big cottony flakes**.

写下雪如此，堪称形象。改译如下：

Light Snow　Qing Jiang

Snowflakes dancing in the wind: a sightly

sight; all of them vanish into forests

and mountains. A doleful man

is standing at the study

window: the snow is

> coming down in big
>
> cottony flakes, one
>
> after another flake
>
> of coldness.
>
> （张智中　译）

（70）观游鱼（白居易）

白居易的这首诗，颇具情趣，值得玩味。

观游鱼　白居易	**Watching Fish Swimming**　Bai Juyi
绕池闲步看鱼游， 正值儿童弄钓舟。 一种爱鱼心各异， 我来施食尔垂钩。	Strolling around the pool, 　I watch fish swimming, when I see an angling boat 　which carries some boys. The same love for fish 　with different intentions: I come to feed fish, and they 　to get them by angling. （张智中　译）

"一种爱鱼心各异"，对应英译：The same love for fish with different intentions，似乎这样也挺好。后来读到如下英文句子：

Lady Catherine continued to speak to Darcy about her **thoughts** on Elizabeth's playing.

凯瑟琳夫人继续对达西谈论着自己对伊丽莎白演奏的看法。

Her **thoughts** were of Pemberley all that evening.

一整夜，她的心思都在彭贝利。

Some of them walked about the garden, with great natural beauty which easily banished the least **thought** of weariness.

于是有的人到花园里散步，园中的自然美景叫人困倦顿失。

Perhaps you also have had similar **thoughts**.

你可能也会有同感。

When she awoke the next morning, Elizabeth began to think again about the same **thoughts** which she had fallen asleep to.

　　第二天早晨，伊丽莎白醒来时，她又开始考虑昨晚她一直想到入睡时的同样的事情。

　　读完这些句子，感觉似乎 intentions 目标性过强，用词过分。如果用 thoughts，或许正得其中。特别是最后一个句子中的 the same thoughts，如果反其意而用之，则是 different thoughts。因有改译：The same love for fish with different thoughts。整首诗改译如下：

Watching Fish Swimming　Bai Juyi

Strolling around the pool,

　　I watch fish swimming,

when I see an angling boat

　　which carries some boys.

The same love for fish

　　with different thoughts:

I come to feed fish, and they,

　　to get them by angling.

（张智中　译）

（71）除夜作（高适）

　　英文名词 thoughts，看起来简单，但却 thought-provoking（引人深思）。又想起一首唐诗的英译：

除夜作　高适	**Composed on New Year's Eve**　Gao Shi
旅馆寒灯独不眠， 客心何事转凄然？ 故乡今夜思千里， 霜鬓明朝又一年。	In a lonely hotel a cold candle is sleepless; why the traveler's heart is seized by sorrow? Tonight my hometown is missing me thousands of miles away: frost-templed; tomorrow, another new year. 　　　　　　（张智中　译）

　　读完上引几个含有 thoughts 或 thought 的英文句子之后，总觉得英文名词

thoughts，可在这首诗的英译方面派上用场。"故乡今夜思千里，霜鬓明朝又一年。"高适的这首《除夜作》，感慨颇深。年是新年了，思念，却是仍旧。如果这样思考，可得如下句子：my old thoughts persist into the new year（我陈旧的或一如既往的思念，一直持续到新年）。

这，当然就是《除夜作》的深层感叹。至于动词 persist 与介词 into 的搭配，可见如下三个英文句子：

The effects are stable, and **persist into** adulthood.

所产生的影响是稳定而持续的，一直到成年。

Celia immediately sensed an antagonism between herself and the director of research which would **persist into** the future.

西莉亚立刻感到，研究部主任对她有着某种敌意，而且恐怕不会轻易消失。

Arianism, although weakened, **persisted into** the Middle Ages.

阿里乌斯派，尽管是弱势，在中世纪却还持续。

那么，《除夜作》改译如下：

Composed on New Year's Eve Gao Shi

In a lonely hotel a cold candle is sleepless;

why the traveler's heart is seized

by sorrow? Tonight my home-

town is missing me thousands

of miles away: frost-templed;

tomorrow, a new year

— into which my

old thoughts

persist.

（张智中　译）

改译中，my old thoughts persist into the new year，倒装，变成了 a new year — into which my old thoughts persist.（新年——我的思念却一如既往，持久不衰。）

又读到如下英文：

And then there was that other memory of low-voiced, bitter rows, coming from another room making her feel as she did now, **full of the longing to leave**.

这里，full of the longing to 表示渴望做某事，用语新鲜。

His was as Irish a face as could be found in **the length and breadth of** the homeland he had left so long ago — round, high colored, short nosed, wide mouthed and belligerent.

他那张纯粹爱尔兰型的脸，同他已离别多年的故乡的那些脸一模一样，是圆圆的、深色的、短鼻子，宽嘴巴，满脸好战的神情。

其中，the length and breadth of，意为"处处；到处"。再如：

She has travelled **the length and breadth of** Britain.

她游历了英国各地。

Uncle Henry was a short, pot-bellied, irascible old gentleman with a pink face, **a shock of long silver hair** and an utter lack of patience with feminine timidities and vaporings.

亨利叔叔是个性情暴戾老绅士，矮个儿，大肚子，脸孔红红的，一头蓬乱的银白长发，他非常看不惯那种女性的怯弱和爱说大话的习惯。

其中，a shock of long silver hair（一头蓬乱的银白长发），描写形象。

又想起许渊冲对杜甫《望岳》中"决眦入归鸟"的英译：

My eyes are strained to see birds **fleet**.

这里，fleet 意为"跑得快的；快速的"。

借鉴之后，《除夜作》改译如下：

Composed on New Year's Eve　　Gao Shi

A cold candle in a lonely hotel illumines a

solitarily sleepless man. Why is his heart

seized by a touch of sorrow? For the

moment, the length and breadth of

my homeland, thousands of miles

away, is full of longing for me,

a wanderer with a shock of

long silver hair, vainly

seeing, tomorrow,

another new

year fleet.

（张智中　译）

（72）闲居初夏午睡起二绝句（其一）（杨万里）

来看宋人杨万里的这首小诗及其英译：

闲居初夏午睡起二绝句（其一）

梅子留酸软齿牙，芭蕉分绿与窗纱。

日长睡起无情思，闲看儿童捉柳花。

Waking Up From an Early Summer Nap　Yang Wanli

In early summer, the sight of plums is suggestive of a

sour taste which softens my teeth; the plantain tree

waves its leaves against the window, sharing its

greenness. A lengthy day sees me napping and

waking up, my mind still blunt and slow

and, through listless hours, I languidly

watch the children running

and catching at willow

catkins, an idle

play.

（张智中　译）

显然，译文借鉴了下面两个英文句子：

What **idle play** is this with yourself, my heart, **through the listless hours**?

我的心啊，在慵倦的时间里，你和自己玩了什么悠闲的游戏？

I walked slowly along the passage to the door by the archway, **my mind still blunt and slow** as though I had just woken from a long sleep.

我拖着缓慢的步子朝拱形市道旁的门户走去。思想依然迟钝麻木，好比刚从一夜酣睡中苏醒过来。

— 163 —

　　这样一来，译诗深层挖掘，尽力再现原诗婉约之深情。后来，读到美国诗人赖特（James Wright, 1927-1980）的英文诗句：

The cowbells follow one another

Into the distances of the afternoon.

牛铃一声接一声

走进晌午的深处。

（赵毅衡　译）[62]

　　觉得 into the distances of the afternoon 的表述，实在婉转而可爱，于是借来改译：

Waking Up From an Early Summer Nap　Yang Wanli

In early summer, the sight of plums is suggestive of a sour

taste which softens my teeth; the plantain tree dances

its leaves against the window, sharing its greenness.

As the day lengthens into the distances of the

afternoon, I awake to find myself in a slow,

blunt mind, and through listless hours,

I languidly watch the children

running about, catching at

willow catkins

— an idle

play.

（张智中　译）

　　后来，又读到这样一个英文小句：

His life **is full of lazy times**.

他生活闲散。

　　觉得清新可爱，觉得非常契合杨万里此诗"闲居初夏午睡起"之"无情思"、"闲看"的状态。于是，改译如下：

Waking Up From an Early Summer Nap

The sight of plums in early summer, which is full of lazy

62 晏榕，诗的复活：诗意现实的现代构成与新诗学——美国现当代诗歌论衡及引申〔M〕，杭州：浙江大学出版社，2013：185。

times, is suggestive of a sour taste which softens my teeth;

the plantain tree waves its leaves against the window,

sharing its greenness. As the day lengthens into

the distances of the afternoon, I awake to find

myself in a slow, blunt mind, and through

listless hours, I languidly watch the

children running about, catching

at willow catkins

— an idle

play.

（张智中　译）

这样一来，译文更有英诗之味道了。借用英文资源，总能取得良好效果。比较许渊冲的两种英译。

英译一：

After a Nap in Early Summer　Yang Wanli

The juice of mume makes my teeth feel a sourness keen;

Banana leaves share their green with my window screen.

What at after a long daynap can I do with pleasure?

I only watch the kids catch willow down at leisure.[63]

英译二：

Rising After a Siesta in Early Summer　Yang Wanli

The aftertaste of mumes has left my teeth still sour;

Banana leaves diffuse their green to window screen.

Indolent after a siesta of long, long hour,

I watch children catch willow-down. What joyful mien![64]

两相比较，可知尾韵有了变化，译诗用词也就很多不同。不过，风格不变的。英译二最后添加的 What joyful mien，令人感觉唐突。不过，两个译文都大体通顺流畅，完成了诗歌翻译的表意功能。但从英文诗歌的角度，看不出有任何明显的借用或借鉴，与我们借鉴英文之后的英译，大不相同。

---

63 许渊冲，宋元明清诗选：汉英对照［Z］，北京：海豚出版社，2013：79。

64 许渊冲，新编千家诗［Z］，北京：中华书局，2006：129。

（73）无题（李商隐）

无题　李商隐 昨夜星辰昨夜风， 画楼西畔桂堂东。 身无彩凤双飞翼， 心有灵犀一点通。 隔座送钩春酒暖， 分曹射覆蜡灯红。 嗟余听鼓应官去， 走马兰台类转蓬。	**Untitled**　Li Shangyin 　Last night: the brilliant stars and the gentle wind, west of the Painted Tower, east of the Cassia Hall — I chance meet you. Without wings of phoenix, we have no way to fly away to an imaginary place, when we enjoy a complete meeting of the minds and a tacit understanding without the aid of words. We play hook game, and we guess what is covered in the cup under the red candle — the loser to drink wine which is warm and nectarous. Alas! the drumbeat beckons me back to my official duty, in spite of my reluctance; like tumbleweed, I, riding a horse, tumble and stumble on, never to crumble under the weight of a hard life ….
	（张智中　译）

散体英译中，借鉴了如下英文句子：

Dear friend, since we have missed **the brilliant stars** last night, don't we want to miss tonight's?

亲爱的朋友，既然我们错过了昨夜灿烂的星空，难道我们还想错过今晚宁静的夜晚吗？

A **chance meeting** brought the two old friends together again.

偶然的相遇，使两位老朋友重新聚首。

There must be **a complete meeting of the minds**, without any reservations on the part of any member.

每个人的想法都得要完全一致、毫无保留。

We have never said a word, but our minds seem to have reached **a tacit understanding**.

我们没有说过一句话，但我们的心灵好象达成了默契。

The aged peasant is advancing slowly **with the aid of** a cane.

那老农凭借手杖的帮助，慢慢地往前走。

This journey is long and hard. You **stumble** and you **tumble**, but you will never **crumble**.

这是一段漫长又艰难的旅程。你跌跌撞撞，你失足摔倒，但你无法被摧毁。

In this way, we will not advance any more in life **under the weight**

of our emotions and our thoughts.

这样我们就再也不会背着情感和思虑的重压在生命中前进。

如果把李商隐《无题》的散文英译，变成当代英诗的形式，可采取三行译诗对一行原诗，并逐行右缩，形成三行一个单元的格局，并比较许渊冲的译诗。

Untitled Li Shangyin Last night: the brilliant stars 　　and the gentle wind, west 　　　　of the Painted Tower, east of the Cassia Hall — I 　　chance meet you. Without 　　　　wings of phoenix, we have no way to fly away to an 　　imaginary place, when we 　　　　enjoy a complete meeting of the minds and a tacit 　　understanding without 　　　　the aid of words. We play hook game, and we guess 　　what is covered in the cup 　　　　under the red candle — the loser to drink wine, 　　which is warm and nectarous. 　　　　Alas! the drumbeat beckons me back to my official duty, 　　in spite of my reluctance; 　　　　like tumbleweed, I, riding a horse, tumble and stumble 　　on, never to crumble under 　　　　the weight of a hard life …. （张智中　译）	**To One Unnamed**　　Li Shangyin As last night twinkle stars, as last night blows the breeze West of the painted bower, east of Cassia Hall. Having no wings, I can't fly to you as I please; Our hearts at one, your ears can hear my inner call. Maybe you're playing hook in palm and drinking wine Or guessing what the cup hides under candle red. Alas! I hear the drum call me to duties mine; Like rootless weed to Orchid Hall I ride ahead. （许渊冲　译）[65]

65 许渊冲，唐诗三百首：汉英对照 ［Z］，北京：海豚出版社，2013：197。

（74）自嘲（鲁迅）

自嘲　鲁迅	**Self-Mockery**　Lu Xun
运交华盖欲何求，	There's nothing you can do about a hostile fate:
未敢翻身已碰头。	You bump your head before you even turn.
破帽遮颜过闹市，	When in the street I pull my old hat down;
漏船载酒泛中流。	My leaky wine-boat drifts along the torrent.
横眉冷对千夫指，	Coolly I face a thousand pointing fingers,
俯首甘为孺子牛。	Then bow to be an infant's willing ox.
躲进小楼成一统，	Hiding in our little house, sufficient to ourselves,
管他冬夏与春秋。	I care not what the season is outside.
	（詹纳尔 W. J. F. Jenner 译）[66]

　　译文虽然整体很好，但有局部问题。例如，在人称方面，使用了 you, I (my), our (ourselves)。其实，原诗只是一个人称，而译诗却变成了"你"、"我"、"我们"三种人称，单数和复数的混用，导致人称方面的混乱。另外，"躲进"，当真 Hiding（躲藏）乎？躲什么？为什么躲？——其实，这里的"躲"，乃是隐居之意。因此，下面的两个英译都采用 seclude，正得其中。最后，詹纳尔的译文，在英语的借用方面，似无明显之痕迹。

　　再来看中国文学出版社未署名译者的译文，以及笔者的译文：

A Satire on Myself　Lu Xun	**Self-Mockery**　Lu Xun
Born under an unlucky star,	Ill-fated under an unlucky star, what can I do?
What could I do?	Attempting to shed it off, I get a blow on the head.
Afraid to turn a somersault,	An old hat to screen off my face, I cut through the crowd,
Still my head received a blow.	Like drinking alone in a lonely leaking boat.
My face hidden under a torn hat,	Glaring angrily at those universally condemned,
I cross the busy market.	I am ready to be the willing ox of common people.
Carrying wine in a leaking boat,	Self-willed, I seclude myself in my own room,
I sail downstream.	To be in some self-satisfied world of my own.
Eyebrows raised, coldly confronting	（张智中　译）
Accusing fingers of a thousand bullies.	
Yet with my head bowed,	

---

66 鲁迅著，（英）詹纳尔（W. J. F. Jenner）译，鲁迅诗选：汉英对照［Z］，北京：外文出版社，2016：31。

I'll be an ox for children. Secluded in my small attic, I'll enjoy my solitary state. Who cares if it's winter or summer? Who cares if it's autumn or spring? （中国文学出版社　译）[67]	

中国文学出版社的译文，采取一行双译，这也是古诗英译的常见现象。其中，Afraid to turn a somersault（不敢翻跟头），这样来理解和英译"未敢翻身已碰头"之"未敢翻身"，一般也就国外学者如此，中国学者一般不至于做如此之字面理解。不过，随后的 Still my head received a blow，却是很好的英文表达，又是一般中国译者所译不出来的。

在笔者的英文中，I cut through the crowd，是借用英文而来的好句子。"千夫指"，对应英文 those universally condemned，是联想到英文名著《傲慢与偏见》中的名句 it is a truth universally acknowledged that ...，然后化用而来。最后两行中的 self-willed 和 self-satisfied，来自下面两个英文句子：

... you **self-willed** creature.

你这个犟丫头！

She was in some **self-satisfied world of her own**.

她有自己的世界，很惬意。

这里, self-satisfied world, 大好：既押头韵，又表意凝练。同时, self-satisfied 又与其上的 self-willed 形成同源关系，更促进了译诗之诗意。

外文出版社的《出版前言》写道："我们意识到，这些翻译精品，不单有对外译介的意义，而且对国内外语学习者、爱好者及翻译工作者，也是极有价值的读本。为此，我们对这些翻译精品做了认真的遴选，编排成中外对照的形式，陆续出版，以飨读者。"[68]

欲出翻译精品，当然不是一件简单的事情。除了要做到正确理解，甚至深度理解之外，我们认为，汉诗英译必须有英语味。而这英语味，在很大程度上来自对原创英文的借鉴。

---

67 中国文学出版社编，中国文学：现代诗歌卷（汉英对照）[Z]，北京：中国文学出版社，1998：7。

68 鲁迅著，（英）詹纳尔（W. J. F. Jenner）译，鲁迅诗选：汉英对照 [Z]，北京：外文出版社，2016。

（75）社日（王驾）

社日　王驾 鹅湖山下稻粱肥， 豚栅鸡栖半掩扉。 桑柘影斜春社散， 家家扶得醉人归。	**Sacrificial Day for Local God**　Wang Jia Beneath Ehu Mountain crops are growing well; the doors of pigsties and hen-coops are half-closed. Mulberry trees are lengthening their shadows when the banquet disperses; tipsy drunkards are helped home by their family members. （张智中　译）

译文也算合格。但是，后来读到爱尔兰作家斯托克（Bram Stoker）的英文小说《德古拉》，里面有如下两个英文句子，顿时眼睛一亮：

The crowd **melted away**.

人群散开了。

Already the sudden storm is passing, and its fierceness is abating; **crowds are scattering homeward**.

突如其来的暴风雨慢慢地减弱了，人群渐渐散去。

在后来的英文阅读中，又读到类似的句子：

Crows **scattered from trees** with a clatter of wings.

同样，用 scatter 表示散开。

这样描写人群散开归去，正吻合"家家扶得醉人归"之意。借用地道之英文，改译如下：

The Spring Sacrificial Banquet Day　Wang Jia

Beneath the Goose-Lake Mountain, there are bumper

farm crops; pigsties, henroosts, all behind wicket

gates ajar. The shadows of mulberry trees are

lengthening and fading, in which crowds

of villagers, tipsy from the sacrificial

banquet, are melting away,

scattering homeward,

in twos and

threes.

（张智中　译）

改译多处，其中，"家家扶得醉人归"的英译：crowds of villagers, tipsy from the sacrificial banquet, are melting away, scattering homeward, in twos and threes. 译文形象生动。再看原译：tipsy drunkards are helped home by their family members. 字面忠实，却无文采。借用英文之后的改译，总能出彩。

（76）辛夷坞（王维）

辛夷坞　王维 木末芙蓉花， 山中发红萼。 涧户寂无人， 纷纷开且落。	**The Magnolia Retreat**　Wang Wei Magnolia flowers in a tree bloom red in deep mountain. Hills and rills are deserted and still: the tree comes into blossoms, only to fall. （张智中　译）

这样英译也可以了。但反复读之，总觉得有点若有所失。偶然读到这个英文句子：

A cherry tree stood in a dress of blossoms, and as the wind took up **it loosened a drift of petals** like confetti.

路旁的樱桃树站在厚厚的一裙花云里，一阵风吹过，便洒下一地五彩的糖果纸。

其中，it loosened a drift of petals，译为汉语，大概如此："树枝松懈了一下，便飘荡出纷纷的花瓣。"多美的语言！不正是"纷纷开且落"的状貌吗？改译如下：

The Magnolia Retreat　Wang Wei

Magnolia flowers in a tree

bloom red in deep mountain.

Hills and rills are deserted

and still: the tree comes

into blossoms, before

it loosens a drift

of petals.

（张智中　译）

（77）春女怨（朱绛）

唐人朱绛的《春女怨》，虽然不太有名，但却描写形象。

春女怨　朱绛	Complaint of a Spring Lady　Zhu Jiang
独坐纱窗刺绣迟， 紫荆花下啭黄鹂。 欲知无限伤春意， 尽在停针不语时。	Sitting alone by screen window, in embroidery she is slow; among redbuds orioles twitter on and on. O, her boundless sentimental feelings about spring are descried in her trance where no needlework is done. （张智中　译）

后来，读到这样一个英文句子：

He obeyed, in the old mechanically submissive manner, **without pausing in his work**.

他服从了，是以前那种机械的、驯服的方式看他，却没有停止他的工作。

其中，pausing in his work（停止他的工作），非常形象。其实，pausing，表示暂停之意，比之 stop 或上译 no needlework is done，要好多了。改译如下：

Complaint of a Spring Lady　Zhu Jiang

Sitting alone by screen
　　window, in embroidery
she is slow; among redbuds
　　orioles twitter on and on.
O, her boundless sentimental
　　feelings about spring are
descried in her trance:
　　a pause in her needlework.

（张智中　译）

改译 a pause in her needlework（她暂停手中的针线活），把 pause 用作 trance 的同位语：暂停手中的针线活，这就是出神（trance）。译文显有进步。

（78）观书有感（其一）（朱熹）

宋代名家朱熹的哲理诗及其英译：

观书有感（其一）　朱熹 半亩方塘一鉴开， 天光云影共徘徊。 问渠那得清如许， 为有源头活水来。	**On Reading**　Zhu Xi A square pond opens like a mirror, on which the sky-light and shadows of clouds are throwing patterns. Why should the water be so clear and clean? Because it has a running headspring. （张智中　译）

译文中，on which the sky-light and shadows of clouds are throwing patterns，借鉴了下面这个英文句子：

The mist was breaking, the sun was forcing its way through and **throwing patterns on the carpet**.

阳光透过渐渐消散的迷雾，在地毯上投下一幅幅图案。

后来，又读到下面两个英文句子：

The sea stretched before her, **a giant expanse of deep blue**, …

He was enchanted by **the intoxicating loveliness** of the night.

这里，a giant expanse of deep blue 和 the intoxicating loveliness 的搭配，感觉新奇而有魅力，总觉得可以用上朱熹的这首《观书有感》。几经周折，改译如下：

On Reading　Zhu Xi

A square pond spreads like a mirror,

over which sky-light and shadows

of clouds are throwing patterns:

an expanse of intoxicating

loveliness. Why should

the water be so clear

and clean? Because

it has a running

　　　　　　　　headspring.

　　　　　　　　（张智中　译）[69]

　　其中，改译的 an expanse of intoxicating loveliness（一片迷人的可爱景色），
似乎成为译文的语言亮点，令人陶而醉之。比读许渊冲的英译：

The Book　Zhu Xi

There lies a glassy oblong pool,

Where light and shade pursue their course.

How can it be so clear and cool?

For water fresh comes from its source.[70]

　　许译尾韵完美，音节整齐，做到了译诗音美上的忠实，但就诗歌语言的新
颖度而言，因为较少借用英文的"优质资源"，而缺乏了点"源头活水"。

（79）病牛（李纲）

病牛　李纲	**A Sick Cow**　Li Gang
耕犁千亩实千箱， 力尽筋疲谁复伤？ 但得众生皆得饱， 不辞羸病卧残阳。	ploughs and ploughs until a bumper harvest; weary from the heavy workload: who is to pity you? In order for each and every person to be well-fed, the sick cow chooses to collapse in the setting sun. （张智中　译）

　　读英文：

　　　　The country of the Quadlings seemed rich and happy. There was
field upon field of ripening grain, with well-paved roads running
between, and pretty rippling brooks with strong bridges across them.

　　　　奎特林这个地方似乎非常富裕、幸福。这里有一片片成熟的稻
田，平坦的道路横亘其中，潺潺流动的溪流上面驾着坚固的桥梁。

---

69 张智中，宋诗绝句 150 首：今译及英译：汉英对照［Z］，武汉：武汉大学出版社，
2021：50。

70 许渊冲，宋元明清诗选：汉英对照［Z］，北京：海豚出版社，2013：80-81。

这里，field upon field，写一片片田野，非常形象。

> But **acres on acres** full of such patriarchs contiguously rooted, their green tops billowing in the wind, their stalwart younglings pushing up about their knees: a whole forest, healthy and beautiful, giving colour to the light, giving perfume to the air: what is this but the most imposing piece in nature's repertory?

> 一亩接一亩的树族的长者稳稳地矗立在那儿，头顶繁茂的枝叶在风中翻滚，它们健壮的后代簇拥着生长在它们膝边：整片森林，孕育着美丽和健康，给阳光增色不少，也给空气添加了芳香。这是大自然上演的剧目中最让人心动的一幕。

这里，acres on acres，一亩接一亩，正可用来描写"耕犁千亩实千箱"之"千亩"。

> Melly **collapsed** into tears and laid her head on the pillow.

> 媚兰又泪流满面，把头倒在枕头上哭了起来。

这里的动词 collapse，也可描写"不辞羸病卧残阳"之病牛。整首诗改译如下，并比较许渊冲的译诗：

A Sick Cow Li Gang	**To a Sick Buffalo** Li Gang
ploughs acres on acres, in field upon field of ripening grain; weary from the heavy workload: who is to pity you? In order for people to be well-fed, the sick cow is ready to collapse in the setting sun. （张智中　译）	You've ploughed field on field and reaped crop on crop of grain. Who would pity you when you are tired out and done? If old and young could eat their fill, then you would fain Exhaust yourself and lie sick in the setting sun.[71] （许渊冲　译）

笔者的译文中，再次使用了跨题的技巧：动词 ploughs 的主语，正是译诗的标题 A Sick Cow。整体而言，译诗舍弃了原诗的音美和形美——其实，不是舍弃，而是背离。原诗四行，且押尾韵，译诗八行，没有尾韵。但在译诗中，两个 acres 和两个 field 的使用，介词 on 与 upon 押单词尾韵，weary 与 heavy 押单词尾韵，workload 与 who 押单词头韵，同时，who 与 you 又押单词尾韵，

---

[71] 许渊冲，宋元明清诗选：汉英对照［Z］，北京：海豚出版社，2013：70。

sick，setting，sun 押单词头韵，cow 与 collapse 押单词头韵，韵律感还是比较
明显的。译者放弃了汉语诗歌之韵，却再创了译诗之韵。就形美而言，显然，
译者放弃了古诗的整齐之美，却再建了英诗的倒三角形之美。许渊冲的译诗，
一般都是在忠于原诗音美和形美的前提下，努力达至意美的境界。

（80）过华清宫绝句三首（一）（杜牧）

过华清宫绝句三首（一）　杜牧 长安回望绣成堆， 山顶千门次第开。 一骑红尘妃子笑， 无人知是荔枝来。	**Three Quatrains of Huaqing Palace (No. 1)**　Du Mu From the capital looking back at Lishan Mountain, which is filled with piles of embroidery; atop the mountain thousands of doors open one after another. At the sight of galloping horses, the imperial concubine laughs: nobody knows the load is litchi, her favorite. （张智中　译）

译完不久，读到英文小说《飘》（Gone with the Wind）里的句子：

The red road lay checkered in shade and sun-glare beneath the over-
arching trees and the many hooves **kicked up little red clouds of dust**.

阳光在枝柯如拱的大树下闪烁，那条红土大道在树荫中光影斑
驳，纷纷而过的马蹄扬起一阵阵云雾般的红色尘土。

这里描写的不正是"一骑红尘"吗？

至于"妃子笑"，《飘》中的另一个句子：

She **laughed like everything** when we told her about it.

我们告诉她这消息时，她笑得不行。

其中，短语 like everything，意为"猛烈地；拼命地"。

那么，《过华清宫绝句三首（一）》改译：

Three Quatrains of Huaqing Palace (No. 1)　Du Mu

From the capital looking back at Lishan Mountain,

which is fair with piles of embroidery; atop the

mountain thousands of doors open one after

another. At the sight of a galloping horse,

whose hooves kick up little red clouds

of dust, the imperial concubine

laughs like everything:

nobody knows the

load is litchi, her

favorite.

（张智中　译）

后来，又读到两句英文：

And **wreaths of dust were spinning round and round** before the morning blast, as if the desert-sand had risen far away, and the first spray of it in its advance had begun to overwhelm the city.

在晨风刮起之前，一圈圈的灰尘已经不停地翻滚起来，仿佛沙漠的黄沙已经在远处飘扬，它的先锋部队已经开始笼罩着这座城市。

句中，wreaths of dust were spinning round and round，若用来英译"一骑红尘"，则形象顿生。

Walk in the woods, and the dry leaves rustle with the whir of their wings, **the air is vocal with their cheery call**.

走在树林中，会听到落叶伴着他们的翅膀的嗖嗖声，刷刷作响。

空气中弥漫着他们愉悦的叫声。

这里，the air is vocal with their cheery call，若稍作改动，用来英译妃子笑声之爽朗，在空气中回荡，则译文又传其神。因此，改译如下：

Three Quatrains of Huaqing Palace (No. 1)　Du Mu

Back view from the capital at Lishan Mountain,

which is filled with piles of embroidery; atop

the mountain thousands of doors open one

after another. At the sight of galloping

horses through wreaths of dust which

are spinning round and round, the

imperial concubine laughs,

and the air is vocal with

her cheery laughter —

nobody knows the

load is litchi, her

favorite.

（张智中　译）

改译之后，又读到一个相关的英文句子：

The cavalcade came prancing along the road, with a great clattering of hoofs and a mighty cloud of dust, which rose up so dense and high that the visage of the mountain-side was completely hidden from Ernest's eyes.

马队沿着大路昂首阔步，蹄声山响，烟尘滚滚，烟尘扬得又高又厚，欧内斯特连山坡上的人面巨石都完全看不见了。

真是巧合，似乎正是"一骑红尘"的英文版了。借鉴英文资源，再次散体改译如下：

Back view from the capital at Lishan Mountain, which is filled with piles of embroidery; atop the mountain thousands of doors open one after another. The cavalcade come prancing along the road, with a great clattering of hoofs and a mighty cloud of dust, which rises up so dense and high that the visage of the mountain is completely hidden from the eyes of the imperial concubine with whose cheery laughter the air is vocal — nobody knows the load is litchi, her favorite.

诗体排列如下：

Three Quatrains of Huaqing Palace (No. 1)　　Du Mu

Back view from the capital at Lishan Mountain,

which is filled with piles of embroidery; atop

the mountain thousands of doors open one

after another. The cavalcade come prancing

along the road, with a great clattering

of hoofs and a mighty cloud of dust,

which rises up so dense and high

that the visage of the mountain

is completely hidden from the

eyes of the imperial concubine

with whose cheery laughter

the air is vocal — nobody

knows the load is litchi,

her favorite.

（张智中　译）

这样一来，译文更加生动传神。比读许渊冲的译诗：

The Summer Palace　Du Mu

Viewed from afar, the hill's paved with brocades in piles;

The palace doors on hilltops opened one by one.

A steed which raised red dust won the fair mistress' smiles.

How many steeds which brought her fruit died on the run!72

如果仔细追究，the hill's paved with brocades in piles（山用一堆堆的丝绸砌成），感觉不太自然。"山顶千门"之"门"，当用 gate，而不是 door。"一骑红尘妃子笑"对应英文：A steed which raised red dust won the fair mistress' smiles，翻译痕迹明显；"无人知是荔枝来"英译：How many steeds which brought her fruit died on the run！虽然译文跳脱，但似乎并未增进译诗的内在情感。缺乏英文语言精华的借鉴，总觉得译文贫血，少了点活力。

（81）山中问答（李白）

山中问答　李白	**In the Mountain: Reply to a Question**　Li Bai
问余何意栖碧山， 笑而不答心自闲。 桃花流水窅然去， 别有天地非人间。	You ask why I live in the green mountain? I smile back as a reply, light-hearted and easy of mind. Peach blossoms gone with running water: for me, this is a paradise. 　　　　（张智中　译）

晨读英文，读到这样的句子：

72 许渊冲，唐诗三百首：汉英对照［Z］，北京：海豚出版社，2013：178-179。

Elinor looked surprised at his emotion; but trying to **laugh off the subject**, she said to him …

埃莉诺见他如此激动，感到非常惊讶，不过还是尽量想笑一笑，岔开话题，就对他说……

总觉这里的 laugh off 有些可爱，甚合李太白"笑而不答"之意。于是改译如下：

In the Mountain: Reply to a Question　Li Bai

"Why should you live

in the green mountain?"

with a light heart at ease,

I laugh off the question.

Peach blossoms gone

with running water:

this is a paradise

for me.

（张智中　译）

后来，又读到两个英文句子：

The air tinkled with her laughter.

"笑而不答"，英译中似可这样处理：the air is tinkling with my laughter。

另一个句子：

This was heaven: to be together in happy stillness.

共处平静，同享喜乐，人间即是天堂。

这正是"别有天地非人间"的英文呼应，似乎照搬即可。因此，又译如下：

In the Mountain: Reply to a Question　Li Bai

Asked why I choose to live in green mountain,

I smile back as a reply, the air tinkling

with my laughter: light-hearted

and easy of mind. Peach

blossoms gone with

running water —

for me, this is

heaven: to be

together in

happy still-

ness.

（张智中　译）

不过，这还没完。后来又读到几个好的英文句子，包括霍克斯英译《红楼梦》第七回中的句子：

> 二人一样胡思乱想。宝玉又问他读什么书，秦钟见问，便依实而答。二人你言我语，十来句话，越觉亲密起来了。

> Each, plunged in reverie, for a while said nothing. Then Bao-yu asked Qin Zhong about his reading, and Qin Zhong replied — **a full, frank reply**, without the trappings of politeness: and presently they were in the midst of a delightful conversation and were already like old friends.

译文中，a full, frank reply，两个单词押头韵，简单而有韵味。另一个英文句子：

> …and **his whole face beams with an ecstatic smile**.

> 满脸洋溢着异常欣喜的微笑。

两相结合，似可用来英译李白的"笑而不答"：I give a full, frank reply, my whole face beaming with an ecstatic smile。

第三个英文句子：

> Salabetto **supposed himself to be in paradise**, for he had never before enjoyed such a delicate feast.

> 萨拉巴托觉得自己简直就是置身天堂，因为他从未享受过如此待遇。

联想到李白的"别有天地非人间"，似可如此英译：I suppose myself to be in paradise（我觉得自己简直就是置身天堂。）那么，李白《山中问答》再次改译如下：

In the Mountain: Reply to a Question　Li Bai

Asked why I choose to live in green mountain,

I give a full, frank reply, my whole face

beaming with an ecstatic smile,

the air tinkling with my laughter.

I, light-hearted and easy of mind,

suppose myself to be in paradise,

where peach blossoms

are wafting with

running

water

....

（张智中　译）

经过一段时间的阅读，又积累了一些相关的英文句子：

Alice was thoroughly puzzled. 'Does the boots and shoes!' she repeated **in a wondering tone**.

艾丽丝完全被弄迷糊了。"擦靴子和鞋子！"她疑惑地重复道。

The Mouse only growled **in reply**.

老鼠只是嘟囔了一声，算是回答。

He wheeled round upon his stool, with a steaming test tube in his hand and **a gleam of amusement in his deepset eyes**.

他在圆凳上转过身来，手里拿着那支冒气的试管，深陷的眼睛里流露出微微的笑意。

At first **his countenance was illuminated with pleasure**, but as he continued, thoughtfulness and sadness succeeded; at length, laying aside the instrument, he sat absorbed in reflection.

起初，他脸上洋溢着笑容，但弹着弹着，表情便变得深邃、忧伤。最后，他把吉他搁置一旁，坐在那里沉思着。

No more does his infernal **laugh go echoing among the hills**, and no more does his fat moon-face rise up to vex me.

他那可恶的笑声再也不会在山间回响，他那圆月般的胖脸也不会再在我面前升起，惹我心烦。

Alf felt himself grow hot all over **at the hateful words** "pay now."

当听到"现在付钱"这几个讨厌的字时，阿尔夫觉得自己浑身发热。

The sound of their voices wafted across the lake to us.

他们的声音飘过湖面传到我们这里。

A slip, and to right or left the man would fall to his death. But once across **he would find himself in an earthly paradise**.

一个人向左或者向右一滑都会摔死。但是一旦通过了，他就会发现自己到了人间天堂。

汲取以上英文相关表达，采取当代英诗常见建行格式，《山中问答》另译如下：

In the Mountain: Reply to a Question   Li Bai

"Why should you live in the green

　　mountain?" You ask me in a

　　　　wondering tone. I smile in reply,

my eyes with a gleam of amuse-

　　ment, my countenance illuminated

　　　　with pleasure, my heart light and

my mind easy —— my laughter

　　goes echoing among the hills.

　　　　At which peach blossoms waft

with running water across the

　　lake to the horizon, when I find

　　　　myself in an earthly paradise.

（张智中　译）

再看相关的英文积累：

At this word excuses a cloud passed over the brow of Athos, a haughty smile curled the lip of Porthos, and **a negative sign was the reply of Aramis**.

听到道歉这两个字，阿托斯的眉间顿现一片乌云，波尔托高傲地笑了笑，阿拉米则表现得不以为然。

At these words she passed her arm under that of D'Artagnan, and pulled him forward eagerly.

说着，她一把挎起达塔尼昂的胳膊，拽着他想赶紧走。

D'Artagnan approached the young men with a profound bow, accompanied by **a most gracious smile**.

达塔尼昂于是向这几个年轻人走去，满面笑容地朝他们深深地鞠了一躬。

Moving up the road I gazed about **with a delightful feeling of leisure**.

上路之后，我环顾四周，感到悠闲自在。

Here is **the fruit of my leisured ease**, the magnum opus of my latter years!

这是我悠闲自在的成果，这就是我近年来的代表作！

This is a village **remote from the madding crowd**.

这是一个远离喧嚣尘世的村庄。

Agatha asked **a question, to which the stranger only replied by pronouncing**, in a sweet accent, the name of Felix.

阿加莎过去询问她，这个陌生人只是声音甜美地说出了弗利克斯的名字。

He answered her by the warm light in his eyes.

他眼睛里流露出充满温情的目光算作回答她。

"You will go south?" said Gerald, **a little ring of uneasiness in his voice**.

"去南方吗？"杰拉德有点不安地问。

But when Mapuhi exposed the pearl to his sight he managed to suppress the startle it gave him, and **to maintain a careless, commercial expression on his face**.

不过，当马普希给他看那颗珍珠的时候，他还是设法克制住了内心的惊讶，脸上保持着一副生意人的漫不经心的表情。

He answered the appeal of his friend **by an affirmative nod of the head**.

对于朋友的问话，他点了点头表示肯定。

The unknown looked at him for a moment longer **with his faint smile**, and retiring from the window, came out of the hostelry with a slow step, and placed himself before the horse within two paces of D'Artagnan.

那个陌生人微微笑着又看了他一会儿，然后离开窗口，慢慢地踱出客店，来到离达塔尼昂两步远的地方，面对着马站定。

Athos, whose keen eyes lost nothing, **perceived a sly smile pass over the lips of the young Gascon as he replied**.

什么都逃不过阿托斯的眼睛，这时，他看见这个加斯科涅人的嘴边掠过了一丝难以察觉的微笑。

汲取如上英文表达，《山中问答》又有两种英译：

Question & Reply in the Mountain Li Bai "Why should you dwell in the green mountain?" At this question, a gracious smile is my reply, with a delightful feeling of leisured ease. Away, away with running water: peach flowers afloat flow afar — to the far horizon, an earthly paradise, which is remote from the madding crowd. （张智中　译）	Question & Reply in the Mountain Li Bai "Why should you dwell in the green mountain?" To the question I only reply by a smile from easiness of mind, with warm light in my eyes. Away, away with running water: peach flowers afloat flow afar — to the far horizon, an earthly paradise, which is remote from the madding crowd. （张智中　译）

又读到一句英文：

And **something like a faint smile glided over** the still terrified features of the young woman.

在这位年轻太太惊魂未定的脸上，隐约露出了一抹淡淡的微笑。

对于笑容的描写，形象生动而细节毕现。"笑而不答心自闲"的英译，似可借鉴：

At this question, something like a faint smile glides over my face.

因此，只要我们不断坚持英文阅读，一首汉语古诗的译文似乎也就没有终止的时候。

（82）诗经·采薇

我们来看《诗经》中的名句，并比较其英译：

行道迟迟，载渴载饥。 我心伤悲，莫知我哀！ （《诗经·采薇》）	Hunger and thirst Press me the worst. My grief o'erflows. Who knows? Who knows? （许渊冲　译）[73]	The homeward march is slow; My hunger and thirst grow. My heart is filled with sorrow; Who on earth will ever know! （汪榕培　译）[74]

我们读到这样的英文句子：

He **dragged his feet**.

他一步步向前挪着步子。

He **staggered** into the road, **his face thick with grief**.

他蹒跚着回到路上，满面悲痛。

After speaking to Maureen, **his steps had grown heavier**.

和莫琳通话后，他的脚步变沉了。

这三个英文句子，显然可以借鉴，用来翻译《诗经》中的这四行。经过一番琢磨，可得如下两种英译：

Staggering, I drag my feet along the way, stricken with thirst and hunger. My face is thick with grief, and my heart, heavy with sorrow. （张智中　译）	Staggering, I drag my feet — stricken with thirst and hunger — along the way, my face thick with grief, my heart heavy with sorrow, and my steps growing heavier — and heavier. （张智中　译）

后来，又读到这个英文句子：

He **walked through wind and weather, and beneath sun-bleached skies**.

狂风暴雨挡不住他的脚步，阳光炙烤下他依然不停前行。

觉得用来英译上引之《诗经》名句，同样贴切，于是便有第三种英译：

Walking through wind and weather,

beneath sun-bleached skies, I fall

prey to thirst and hunger. Heavy grows

73　许渊冲，诗经（汉英对照）[Z]，长沙：湖南出版社，1993：321。
74　汪榕培、任秀桦，诗经：中英文版 [Z]，沈阳：辽宁教育出版社，1995：693。

my walking, and my heart. Oh my!

（张智中　译）

最后的 my，乃是感叹词，表示"天呢！"之意。一行之中，三用 my，且含义有所流变，增进了音美和意美。另外，第一行中，wind 与 weather 押头韵；第二行中，beneath 与 bleached，sun 与 skies 分别押头韵，而 skies 又与 I 押元音韵；第三行中，hunger 与 heavy 押头韵，thirst 与 hunger 押元音韵。因此，四行译诗虽然没有尾韵，却同样韵律盎然。

再来与原诗比较："行道迟迟，载渴载饥。我心伤悲，莫知我哀！"英译不是字面上的对应，而是深层含义上的呼应。而且，有了介词 through，sun-bleached skies，I fall prey to，以及一唱三叹的 my，译文向英文靠拢，接近地道的英诗。

其实，饥渴伤悲，乃是人生常见之现象，如果坚持英文阅读，便可读到相关的好句子。另如下面例句：

…the road along which **I was moving with wearied feet**.

我迈着沉重的步伐，沿着这条路往前走。

The keenness of his hunger had departed.

强烈的饥饿感也消失了。

The hunger pangs were sharp.

饥饿的阵痛非常剧烈。

To whom shall I tell my grief?

我该向谁述说我的忧伤？

She couldn't think what exactly it was, other than **an unspecific weight of pain**.

除了沉甸甸的痛，她想不到还有什么结束了。

这里的 unspecific，"难以名状"之意。

那么，"行道迟迟，载渴载饥。我心伤悲，莫知我哀！"又可英译如下：

I am moving with wearied feet along the road,

while feeling a constant keenness of hunger when

my thirst and hunger pangs are sharp. An unspecific

weight of pain　——　my grief, to whom shall I tell?

（张智中　译）

再读相关之英文句子：

With drooping heads and tremulous tails, they **mashed their way through the thick mud, floundering and stumbling between whiles.**

他们踏着泥泞的道路向前跋涉，时不时地挣扎一下。

这里描写的是动物，但如果写人，也完全可以。正可绘"行道迟迟"之状貌。

A disturbed and doleful mind he **brought to bear upon** them, and **slowly and heavily the day lagged on with him.**

他为她们又是着急又是痛苦，日子过得极其缓慢沉重。

这里，doleful mind 的搭配很好，可用来英译"我心伤悲"；slowly and heavily the day lagged on with him，可用来改译"行道迟迟"。

The stomachs would have been **more famine-pinched**.

此句若用来英译"载渴载饥"，则非常形象。

His misery is immense, beyond all bounds.

他的苦恼无限巨大，漫无边际。

显然，这句话可用来英译"我心伤悲"。

好了，"行道迟迟，载渴载饥。我心伤悲，莫知我哀！"便有了第五种英译：

With a drooping head, I mash my way through the thick
mud, floundering and stumbling between whiles. Slowly
and heavily the day is lagging on with me, when my stomachs
are more and more famine-pinched. A disturbed and doleful
mind I bring to bear upon myself, and my misery is immense,
beyond all bounds —— but, to whom shall I tell?

（张智中　译）

此译显然繁冗。但，与上引许渊冲和汪榕培的英译相比，如此英译，更有英语的味道。其实，这就是许渊冲所倡导的发挥译文的优势。如果我们坚持阅读，并注意留心，总能读到类似的英语句子或表述。可以说，如果没有英文的借用或借鉴，译文往往会显得平淡无味。有了借鉴，译文便可瞬间出彩。

（83）赠汪伦（李白）

赠汪伦	To Wang Lun
李白乘舟将欲行， 忽闻岸上踏歌声。 桃花潭水深千尺， 不及汪伦送我情。	Li Bai is about to depart on a boat, when the sound of singing & stamping comes from ashore. The depth of Peach Blossom Lake is one thousand fathoms, but not so deep as Wang Lun's affection to me. （张智中　译）

后来，读到英文：

From **the depth of** the canyon comes welling silence.

沉寂从深谷中升腾上来。

The depth of his emotion made him vulnerable and she had a feeling that somehow and at some time she so could work upon it as to induce him to forgive her.

他用情很深，使得他容易受到伤害。她有一种感觉，有朝一日，她总能设法利用这一点，劝诱他原谅自己。

It was then he knew **the depth of** his tiredness.

这时候，他才知道自己疲乏到了什么程度。

原译用了 the depth of Peach Blossom Lake，没想到 the depth of the canyon 之外，还可以说 the depth of his emotion 和 the depth of his tiredness。改译如下，译文文字完全相同，做不同的排列：

To Wang Lun　Li Bai	To Wang Lun　Li Bai
Li Bai is about to depart on a boat, when the sound of singing & stamping comes from ashore. The depth of Peach Blossom Lake is one thousand fathoms, but no greater than the depth of Wang Lun's emotion to me. （张智中　译）	Li Bai is about to 　depart on a boat, 　　when the farewell sound of singing 　& stamping comes 　　from ashore. The depth of Peach 　Blossom Lake is 　　one thousand fathoms, but no greater than 　the depth of Wang Lun's 　　emotion to me. （张智中　译）

最后几行的改译：but no greater than the depth of Wang Lun's emotion to me,
译文更加地道，有回味的余地。

（84）黄鹤楼送孟浩然之广陵（李白）

黄鹤楼送孟浩然之广陵 故人西辞黄鹤楼， 烟花三月下扬州。 孤帆远影碧空尽， 唯见长江天际流。	**Seeing My Friend Off at Yellow Crane Tower** My friend leaves the Yellow Crane Tower in the west to Yangzhou in mist-veiled April. His lonely sail sails until it is a mere speck against the boundless blue sky, when Yangtze River is rolling endlessly in the horizon. （张智中　译）

译文中，it is a mere speck 并非笔者的凭空想象，而是根据如下英文句子
化出：

> ... or the **specks** of sail that glinted in the sunlight far at sea.
> 或者又像在远洋中被阳光照耀得闪闪发光的白帆。

> He had been standing on the moor listening to a skylark and
> watching him swing higher and higher into the sky until he was only **a
> speck** in the heights of blue.
> 他站在原野上听一只百灵鸟唱歌，看它在越来越高的天空中盘
> 旋，直到他在蓝天中成为一个小点。

> ... boats were already tiny **flecks** of white.
> 远处河面上的小船已化成白色光点。

名词 fleck，意为"斑点；微粒"，与 speck 之意几乎等同，用来比喻小船
或船帆，甚是恰当。因此，用之英译李白之"孤帆远影碧空尽"，自是贴切。
《黄鹤楼送孟浩然之广陵》是名诗，英译者众多，却很少有人采用 speck 或
fleck。不读英文，则不能如此了。

读凯利、茅国权英译的钱钟书《围城》，发现也有 speck 的运用：

> 衬了这背景，一个人身心的搅动也缩小至于无，只心里一团明
> 天的希望，还未落入渺茫，在广漠澎湃的黑暗深处，一点萤火似的
> 自照着。

> Against this background the tumult in a man's heart shrinks to
> nothingness. Only a well of hope for the morrow, which has not yet
> descended into the vastness, illuminates itself like the **speck** of light from

a firefly in the dark depths of boundless, roaring waves.

那么，如上改译，似乎已经是译诗的完成了。但我们近日却又读到这样一个短语：

On a steaming, misty afternoon.

一个烟雾朦胧的下午。

觉得这里的 steaming, misty，正可绘"烟花三月"之"烟花"之状。因此，再次改译如下：

Seeing My Friend Off at Yellow Crane Tower　Li Bai

My friend leaves the Yellow Crane Tower in the west

to Yangzhou in April when it is steaming, misty

with a variety of flowers. His lonely sail

sails until it is a mere speck against

the boundless blue sky, when

Yangtze River is rolling

endlessly in the

horizon.

（张智中　译）

原译 Yangzhou in mist-veiled April，改译为：Yangzhou in April when it is steaming, misty with a variety of flowers. 这样，感觉好多了。系动词 be 加上形容词，再加上表示原因的介词 with，这种搭配本身，是一种比较诗意的搭配。英文 it is steaming, misty with a variety of flowers 回译汉语："由于繁花盛开，天气显得多香而氤氲，异色而参差。"如此，则诗意大增。

诗歌的翻译，似乎没有完成时。翻译，总在途中。不信，来看这个英文句子：

Far out, a ship travelled the horizon, its lights twinkling, and yet so slow its passage was not visible.

远处海平线上驶过一艘船，灯光明灭，但实在太慢，无法辨认它在往哪个方向航行。

这里，travel 乃是及物动词，意为"到……旅行"。例如词典上的例子：

He travelled Africa last year.

他去年到非洲旅游。

那么，李白《黄鹤楼送孟浩然之广陵》可进一步改译：

Seeing My Friend Off at Yellow Crane Tower　Li Bai

My friend leaves the Yellow Crane Tower in the west

to Yangzhou in April when it is steaming, misty

with a variety of flowers. His boat travels

the horizon, where a lonely sail is sailing

until it is a mere speck against

the boundless blue sky,

when Yangtze River

is rolling endlessly

in the horizon.

（张智中　译）

添加 His boat travels the horizon 之后，语言形象多了。译诗又有进步。比较叶维廉的英译：

To See Meng Hao-jan Off to Yang-chou

My old friend takes off from the Yellow Crane Tower,

In smoke-flower third month down to Yang-chou.

A lone sail, a distant shade, lost in the blue horizon.

Only the long Yangtze is seen flowing into the sky. [75]

（叶维廉　译）

显然，直译为主，很多英文表达都与汉语非常接近。

（85）早春呈水部张十八员外（韩愈）

上引英文短语 on a steaming, misty afternoon.（一个烟雾朦胧的下午。）还可用于韩愈这首名诗的英译：

早春呈水部张十八员外　韩愈	**Early Spring**　Han Yu
天街小雨润如酥，	A slight rain renders the heavenly
草色遥看近却无。	street creamy; green grass
最是一年春好处，	extends afar and is sparse
绝胜烟柳满皇都。	when you approach it.
	It is the fairest view in fair spring

---

75 华满元、华先发，汉诗英译名篇选读［C］，武汉：武汉大学出版社，2014：175。

	of the year: smoky willows veil the imperial capital here and there. （张智中　译）

这里，原译 smoky willows veil the imperial capital here and there，其中的 smoky willows，似乎不是太好。如果改译为 the imperial capital is steaming, misty with willows here and there，则诗意大增。

又读到这么一个英文短语：peppered with bits of green（有了星星点点的绿色），顿时眼睛一亮。英文单词 pepper，作为名词，指"胡椒粉"；作为动词，则是"在……上撒胡椒粉"。自然想起韩愈的"草色遥看近却无"，似可英译：(the field near the heavenly street) is peppered with bits of green。比起原译：green grass extends afar and is sparse when you approach it，要形象多了。整首诗改译如下：

Early Spring　Han Yu

A slight rain renders creamy the heavenly street,

near which the field is peppered with bits

of green. This is the fairest view

in fair spring of the year:

the imperial capital

is steaming, misty

with willows here

and there.

（张智中　译）

如此译诗，已算比较满意。不过，又读到两个英文句子：

The New York **street sparkled in a soft drizzle**.

In the thawed dirt, **bits of green were showing**.

再次改译如下：

Early Spring　Han Yu

The heavenly street sparkles in a soft creamy drizzle,

when bits of green are showing from afar but

disappear on the approach of a traveler.

This is the fairest view in fair spring

of the year: the imperial capital

is steaming, misty with

willows here and

there.

（张智中　译）

在阅读并借鉴英文的同时，笔者另有韩愈《早春呈水部张十八员外》之英译，译诗最后的建行，一时灵感所致，颇有特色，暗示"烟柳满皇都"之袅娜逶迤状貌。

Early Spring　Han Yu

The heavenly street sparkles

in a soft creamy drizzle, when

the field is peppered with bits

of green: showing from afar

but disappearing on the approach

of a traveler. This is the fairest

view in fair spring of the year,

before the imperial capital is

steaming,

misty

with

willows

here

and

there.

（张智中　译）

比较许渊冲的英译：

Early Spring Written for Secretary Zhang Ji　Han Yu

The royal streets are moistened by a creamlike rain;

Green grass can be perceived afar but not near by.

It's the best time of a year that spring tries in vain

With the capital veiled in willows to outvie.[76]

（许渊冲　译）

其中，green grass can be perceived afar but not near by（青草远处可见，走近却不行。）失之平淡，尤其和发挥英文优势的译文相比。许随后的英译 the capital veiled in willows，显然也是套语，陈旧而不新鲜。朱纯深的英译：

Early Spring in the Capital: To Zhang Ji　Han Yu

The fine drizzle has turned the fine streets creamy —

New grass, visible from afar, vanishing when near.

This, my friend, is the best time of the spring, of the year—

Absolutely the best　—　before hazy willows becloud the city.[77]

（朱纯深　译）

"草色遥看近却无"的英译：New grass, visible from afar, vanishing when near（新生之草，远处可见，走进，却消失不见），与许渊冲的英译一样，是忠实通顺的英译。而我们化用英文的英译：the field is peppered with bits of green，或者 bits of green are showing from afar but disappear on the approach of a traveler，显然更具有英文的文学色彩。

再看陈君朴的译文：

An Early Spring Poem Presented To Mr. Zhang, Deputy-Director of Irrigation Department　Han Yu

The drizzle is soft as butter in the streets royal;

Grass, discerned in distance, is not seen near at all.

Now is the best time of the spring in a year, far more

Enchanting than when smoky willows shade the capital.

（陈君朴　译）[78]

为了译文的"忠实"，不惜把标题《早春呈水部张十八员外》直译出来，导致标题冗长。诗行的译文，同样散淡。

76 许渊冲，唐诗三百首：汉英对照［Z］，北京：海豚出版社，2013：120。

77 朱纯深，古意新声：品赏本（汉英对照）［Z］，武汉：湖北教育出版社，2004：100。

78 陈君朴，汉英对照唐诗绝句 150 首［Z］，上海：上海大学出版社，2005：172。

（86）游太平公主山庄（韩愈）

韩愈的另外一首绝句及其英译：

游太平公主山庄　韩愈 公主当年欲占春， 故将台榭押城闉。 欲知前面花多少， 直到南山不属人。	**Visiting the Mountain Villa of Princess Taiping**　Han Yu In time of yore the princess intends to monopolize spring, and her terraces and pavilions outshine city gate. But countless blossoming flowers reach Mt. Zhongnan, which is a place of hermitage. （张智中　译）

诗歌首行"公主当年欲占春"，动词"占"字不好翻译。琢磨半天，用了动词 monopolize，只是感觉还行。后来，读到这样一个英文句子：

Women, in truth, are not only intelligent, they **have almost a monopoly of** certain of the subtler and more utile forms of intelligence.

事实上，女人不仅聪明，而且几乎独占了某些更细致、更实用的智慧形式。

这里的名词 monopoly，与英译的动词 monopolize，具同一意向与情趣。

（87）夏夜（韩偓）

夏夜　韩偓 猛风飘电黑云生， 霎霎高林簇雨声。 夜久雨休风又定， 断云流月却斜明。	**Summer Night**　Han Wo Wild wind, chaotic lightning — black clouds are born. Splashing, splashing in tall woods — the sound of dense rain. Night wears on, rain lets up — wind, too, is settled. Torn clouds — a floating moon once more slants down its light. （Edward H. Schafer 译）

Edward H. Schafer 采取直译法，偶有变通，善用破折号和逗号，译文取得了良好的效果。笔者的英译：

Summer Night　Han Wo

The thunder bursts in tremendous explosions,

when murky clouds are born of wild winds

and flashing lightning, which leaps from

cloud to cloud, and streamed shivering

against the forest tops, splitting and

rending the stoutest trees, raindrops

drizzling and splashing. In the depth

of night the rain stops and the wind

rests, when the flowing moon

gleams aslant behind

the broken

clouds.

（张智中 译）

这是我们坚持英文阅读情况下给出的译文。其中，借鉴了英文小说中的句子：

The lightning leaped from cloud to cloud, and **streamed quivering against the rocks, splitting and rending the stoutest trees. The thunder burst in tremendous explosions;** the peals were echoed from mountain to mountain.

闪电在云层之间穿越，岩石都跟着颤抖起来，树木仿佛要被撕裂一般。雷声接踵而至，在群山间回响着。

再看译诗中的诗行：which leaps from cloud to cloud, and streamed shivering against the forest tops, splitting and rending the stoutest trees, raindrops drizzling and splashing, 显然改写自：The lightning leaped from cloud to cloud, and streamed quivering against the rocks, splitting and rending the stoutest trees。于是，译文深有余味。

（88）长安道（聂夷中）

长安道　聂夷中 此地无驻马， 夜中犹走轮。 所以路傍草， 少于衣上尘。	**Road of the Capital**　Nie Yizhong Here no wagon to station; wheels are day and night running; therefore beside the road grass is less than dust on the robe. （张智中 译）

后来，读到两句英文：

Money alone **sets all the world in motion**.

… it was too quiet, and he needed the **buzz** of the city streets to spark his creative flow.

吸纳借鉴之后，《长安道》改译如下：

Streets of the Capital　Nie Yizhong

Business sets the world in motion: there

is a ceaseless running of wheels day

and night in the streets of the capital,

though without any wagon to

station. The buzz has killed

grass growing by the

streets, and has

filled the robe

with dust.

（张智中　译）

其实，读到英文单词 buzz 等，就联想到了滚滚红尘，而不是"路傍草"和"衣上尘"到底谁多谁少，如何比较衡量。诗歌翻译，靠的是文科思维，即丰富的想象力，而不是一板一眼的理工科思维。诗歌译者应该耽于遐思幻想，而不是精于刻板的计算。

理想的诗歌译者，应该跳脱原文的文字梏，进入诗歌的意境，漫而游之，然后用创作再现的手笔，将内心之所得所悟再现或表达出来。如此这般，翻译才有望取得一定程度上的成功。否则，译文虽然表面忠实，也只是文字上的忠实或对应，诗美早已流失，而译者或读者却不知不觉，叹之悲之。

（89）忆东山二首（一）（李白）

忆东山二首（一）　李白	**Two Poems about the East Mountain (1)**　Li Bai
不向东山久， 蔷薇几度花。 白云还自散， 明月落谁家。	Long time not to the East Mountain, roses blossom and wither time and again. White clouds scatter

	by themselves;
	the bright moon falls
	into which
	courtyard?
	（张智中　译）

后来，读 Donna Dailey 写的 *Charles Dickens* 一书，见到这么一个句子：

The old kidney pains returned as Dickens **dredged up painful memories of** his childhood.

觉得这里的 dredge up painful memories of（勾起……的痛苦记忆），表达非常好。李白此诗中，似可添译：when fond memories are dredged up（当甜美的记忆被勾起）。

整首诗改译如下：

Fond Memories of the East Mountain (No. 1 of two poems)　Li Bai

Absence for a great while from the East

Mountain, where roses blossom and

wither for how many times? White

clouds scatter by themselves;

the bright moon, when

fond memories are

dredged up, now

falls into which

courtyard?

（张智中　译）

（90）红牡丹（王维）

红牡丹　王维	**Red Peony**　Wang Wei
绿艳闲且静，	The peony leaves are quietly and elegantly
红衣浅复深。	green, among which peony petals
花心愁欲断，	exhibit various shades of red.
春色岂知心。	A heart-breaking scene:
	fading, falling, declining,
	decaying …. Spring —
	does spring enjoy

| | the flower's
confidence?
（张智中　译） |

"浅复深"之颜色，翻译出语义不难，但要语言出彩，则比较难。英译 exhibit various shades of red 做到了，因其化用自一个英文句子：

The room was painted **in various shades of blue**.

房间是用深浅不一的蓝色粉刷的。

接下来，fading, falling, declining, decaying，四个连用的现在分词，不仅押尾韵，也押两组头韵，韵律锵然，绘声绘色。译诗最后的用词 confidence，也很用心。来自英文句子：

The servant enjoyed his master's **confidence**.

这仆人深得主人的信赖。

We have full **confidence** that we shall succeed.

我们完全有把握取得成功。

这里的 confidence，意为"信任；把握；信心；知心话"。因此，这里的英译：does spring enjoy the flower's confidence?（春天享受着花儿的信任吗？）这就是"春色岂知心"的委婉表达了。貌离，而神合，总是翻译的最佳状态。

（91）登科后（孟郊）

孟郊的生平快诗及其英译：

| 登科后　孟郊
昔日龌龊不足夸，
今朝放荡思无涯。
春风得意马蹄疾，
一日看尽长安花。 | **After Passing the Imperial Examination**　　Meng Jiao
In time of yore I am down
and have nothing to boast;
now unbridled is my thought
since I have passed imperial
examination. The horse
gallops fast in spring wind;
in a single day I'll admire
all the flowers
in the capital.
（张智中　译） |

后来读到下面的英文句子：

Harold assured her **his son was having the time of his life**.

哈罗德总是告诉她这孩子正是少年得意。

孟郊金榜题名之时，与"少年得意"相仿相佛。另外一个英文句子：

"No," she cried, with triumphant joy. "**It was the complete moment of my life**."

"不，"她凯旋般地叫道，"这是我一生中最得意的时刻。"

因此改译：

After Passing the Imperial Exam   Meng Jiao
In time of yore I am down and have nothing to boast;
now I am having the time, or the complete
moment of my life, since I have passed
the imperial exam. Unbridled is my
mind. The horse gallops fast in
spring wind and, in a single
day I'll admire all the
flowers in the
capital.

（张智中　译）

改译中，把上引两个英文句子的改写进行合并，即把 I am having the time of my life 和 it is the complete moment of my life 合并为一，变成：I am having the time, or the complete moment of my life（我在享受人生最得意的时刻）。这样添译之后，感觉好多了，译文也多了点英语的味道。

又，读 Miss Read 的英文小说 Tyler's Row，见到如下两个句子：

But any slight chagrin was **overwhelmed by the flood of relief which this news brought**. She was going! The cottage would be empty!

"Come and see the vegetable patch," said Peter, when Robert had finished **admiring the flowers**.

根据《登科后》诗意，可如此改写：

Now the news I have passed the imperial examination has brought a flood of relief which overwhelms all my chagrin and ill-humor;

I'll admire all the flowers in the capital。

那么，《登科后》另译如下：

Upon Passing the Imperial Exam　Meng Jiao

In time of yore I am down and out, and nothing

to boast; now the news I've passed the imperial

exam has brought a flood of relief which

overwhelms all my chagrin and ill-

humor: unbridled is my thought.

In spring wind my horse is

galloping and, in a single

day, I'll admire all

the flowers in

the capital.

（张智中　译）

比较许渊冲的英译，及其相关的回译：

Successful at the Civil Service Exam　Meng Jiao Gone are all my past woes! What more have I to say? My body and my mind enjoy their fill today. Successful, faster runs my horse in vernal breeze, I've seen within one day all flowers on the trees.[79] （许渊冲　译）	贺公务员考试成功　孟郊 我过去的痛苦都已过去！我还能说什么呢？ 今天，我的身心都得到巨大的享受。 成功后，我的马在春风中跑得更快， 一天之内,我就看完了树上的花朵！ （张智中　译）

译文当为独立之文本。许渊冲的译诗，回译成汉语，就更清晰了："龌龊"、"不足夸"，语义流失；而"长安花"却变成了语义狭隘的"树上的花朵"。格律体译诗，不仅常有因韵害义之现象，还钳制了诗情的抒发与阐释。

（92）题鹤林寺僧舍（李涉）

题鹤林寺僧舍 终日昏昏醉梦间， 忽闻春尽强登山。	**By a Buddhist Temple** Living a drunken and dreamlike life from day to day, I brace myself

---

79 许渊冲，唐诗三百首：汉英对照［Z］，北京：海豚出版社，2013：116。

因过竹院逢僧话， 又得浮生半日闲。	to climb mountain when spring is on the wane. By a bamboo temple I talk with a monk midway: half a day, in my floating life, is thus whiled away. （张智中　译）

后来，读到这样三个短小的英文句子：

He **detained** them a moment longer.

又唠叨了半日才走开。

They were **chattering together for ages**.

他们咕唧了半日。

So like a fool I spend **half the day** rushing around with her.

我自己多事，为他跑了半日。

就想到这首诗的翻译。随改译如下：

By a Buddhist Temple　Li She

Living a drunken and dreamlike life from day

to day, I brace myself to climb the mountain

when spring is on the wane. By a bamboo

temple I am detained by a monk-friend

midway: chattering together for ages,

half the day, in my floating life,

is thus whiled

away.

（张智中　译）

改译主要在后两行。原译：

By a bamboo temple I talk with a monk midway: half a day, in my
floating life, is thus whiled away.

改译：

By a bamboo temple I am detained by a monk-friend midway:
chattering together for ages, half the day, in my floating life, is thus whiled
away.

语言更加流畅地道。

（93）凉州词二首（二）（王之涣）

凉州词二首（二）　王之涣	**Border Songs (No. 2 of two poems)**　Wang Zhihuan
黄河远上白云间， 一片孤城万仞山。 羌笛何须怨杨柳， 春风不度玉门关。	The Yellow River runs afar into white clouds; a lonely town sits alone amid soaring peaks. Why should the minority flute blame the willows? Spring wind never blows beyond the Jade Gate Pass. （张智中　译）

读到下面的英文句子：

Her hair was **a mass of** tangles.

她的头发乱糟糟的。

Her arm was **a mass of** bruises.

她的胳膊上伤痕累累。

短语 a mass of 表达效果很好。其实，mass 作为名词，更多单独使用，表示"团，块；大量，许多；混乱的一堆"等意思，汉语词汇往往难以对应。例如：

His lips were a contused, shapeless **mass**, and his mouth was full of blood and broken teeth.

他的嘴唇被撞伤了，变成了不成形的一团，而且嘴里满是血和磕坏的牙齿。

Near the horizon the sun was smouldering dimly, almost obscured by formless mists and vapors, which gave an impression of **mass** and density without outline or tangibility.

靠近地平线的地方，太阳在微弱地燃烧着，几乎被无形的雾霭和水汽笼罩住，给人一种没有边际、无法捉摸的庞大而厚重的印象。

In front of them the Lys was rolling its waters like a river of molten lead; while on the other bank could be seen a black **mass** of trees, outlined against a stormy sky, which was invaded by huge coppery clouds, creating a kind of twilight amid the night.

前面利斯河的河水如同融化了的铅水一样翻滚着。河的对岸，

在风雨交加的天空的映衬下，人们只能够看到一片黑压压的树林，
天空中布满了红棕色的乌云，夜晚中的这一切如同暮色一般。

名词的 mass，有时用复数形式，表示强调或夸张，极尽描写一团或一片或一堆混乱无序之物体。例如：

But the woman who sat shook about her great **masses** of dark, wet hair which yielded up its dampness to the warm caresses of the sun.

但是那坐着的女人晃动着一头漆黑、潮湿的头发，发上的湿气接受着太阳温暖的抚摸。

Here and there, at several wide intervals, small **masses** of rock projected through the snow of the slide itself, giving sufficient stability to the enterprise to encourage him.

坡面上到处都是从雪里凸出来的一块块小碎石，相互间隔得距离较宽，这能给他的攀爬带来足够的稳定性，令他很受鼓舞。

A sea of vegetation laved the landscape, pouring its green billows from wall to wall, dripping from the cliff-lips in great vine-**masses**, and flinging a spray of ferns and air-plants in to the multitudinous crevices.

这片风景沐浴在植被的海洋中，碧波从一块块崖壁上倾泻而下，大量的藤蔓从山崖尖上垂下，一簇簇蕨类植物和附生植物伸进群集的岩石裂缝处。

偶然情况下，mass 还可以用作动词，表示"（使）聚集，（使）集结"之意，妙不可言，令人玩味。例如：

Beneath the hill lay the silent city, **massed** confusedly in the twilight of dawn.

寂静的城市躺在山丘下，在破晓的光辉中错落不齐地聚成一片。

因此，"一片孤城万仞山"，背景为一片群山，若考虑使用 mass，则效果必佳。尝试英译：a lonely town sits alone amid **a mass of** soaring peaks.

又读到另外一个英文句子：

But she had just moved there last winter. She hadn't learned how to grow a flower garden yet, so naturally **spring had yet to visit her barren garden**.

可是，从初冬搬倒这里，她还不知道该怎么去栽种花木，园里自然是空空的春风不度。

英文 had yet to，表示应该，但还没有进行的动作。因此，汉语以为"春风不度"，也令人想起"春风不度玉门关"。如果我们化用此一英文句子，可尝试如此英译：Spring wind has yet to visit beyond the Jade Gate Pass。整首诗英译如下，并比较许渊冲的译文：

Border Songs (No. 2 of two poems) Wang Zhihuan The Yellow River runs afar 　　into white clouds; a lonely town sits alone amid a mass of 　　soaring peaks. Why should the minority flute blame the 　　willows which refuse to green? Spring wind has yet to visit 　　beyond the Jade Gate Pass. （张智中　译）	**Out of the Great Wall**　Wang Zhihuan The Yellow River rises to the white cloud; The lonely town is lost amid the mountains proud. Why should the Mongol flute complain no willows grow? Beyond the Gate of Jade no vernal wind will blow. （许渊冲　译）[80]

许渊冲的英译，似乎犯了一个基本常识的错误。凉州：唐陇右道凉州治所在姑臧县（今甘肃省武威市）。羌笛：古羌族主要分布在甘、青、川一带。羌笛是羌族乐器，属横吹式管乐，属于一种乐器。玉门关：汉武帝置，因西域输入玉石取道于此而得名，故址在今甘肃敦煌西北小方盘城，是古代通往西域的要道，六朝时关址东移至今安西双塔堡附近。但是，许译标题 Out of the Great Wall（长城外），和译诗第三行中的 the Mongol flute，说明译者把羌笛误解成蒙古族的笛子了。这个姑且不论，译文在语言上显得平平淡淡，无甚出彩之处。

（94）雁（陆龟蒙）

读到这样一个英文句子：

In the valley, the fields were shrouded in mist.

山下的田野笼罩在暮霭里。

就想起以前英译过的一首唐人绝句：

---

80 许渊冲，唐诗三百首：汉英对照［Z］，北京：海豚出版社，2013：29。

雁　陆龟蒙 南北路何长， 中间万弋张。 不知烟雾里， 几只到衡阳?	**To Geese**　Lu Guimeng The road from north to south is long, above which thousands of arrows to shoot. In dense mist & fog, how many geese can reach Hengyang?* 　（张智中　译） * Translator's note: legend has it that in ancient China, geese in the north fly to the south, with the destination of Hengyang, which is located in Hunan Province.

　　"不知烟雾里"，如果借用上引的英文句子，似可考虑译为 The fields are shrouded in mist。整首诗改译如下：

> **To Geese**　Lu Guimeng
> Long is the road from
> 　　north to south, above
> which thousands of
> 　　arrows are ready to
> shoot. The fields are
> 　　shrouded in mist:
> how many geese can
> 　　safely reach Hengyang?*
> 　（张智中　译）
>
> 　* Translator's note: legend has it that in ancient China, geese in the
> 　north fly southward, with the destination of Hengyang, a city in Hunan
> 　Province.

　　除了借鉴英文句子之外，还有三处改译：第一，把 Long 放在诗歌开头，形成倒装，用来强调。第二，thousands of arrows to shoot，改成 thousands of arrows are ready to shoot，更加形象。第三，how many geese can reach Hengyang? 改成 how many geese can safely reach Hengyang? 添加副词 safely，表意更加充分明细。当然，修改的亮点，还是借鉴英文而来的 The fields are shrouded in mist，后面使用冒号，引出疑问。

（95）九月九日忆山东兄弟（王维）

九月九日忆山东兄弟	**Missing My Brothers on Height-Climbing Day**
独在异乡为异客， 每逢佳节倍思亲。 遥知兄弟登高处， 遍插茱萸少一人。	Alone, a lonely stranger in a strange land, on this Height-Climbing Day I doubly miss my kinsfolk. My mental picture: the cornel wearers at the height of the mountain are my brothers, with me missing .... （张智中　译）

后来，读到这样一个句子：

The poor little thing couldn't **turn her thoughts to** either warming herself or eating.

可怜的小姑娘既不想暖一暖，也不想吃东西。

其中，turn her thoughts to 的表达，感觉婉转可爱。于是改译：

Missing My Brothers on Height-Climbing Day　Wang Wei

Alone, a lonely stranger in a strange land,

on the Height-Climbing Day I turn my

thoughts to my kinsfolk. My mental

picture: the cornel wearers at

the height of the mountain

are my brothers, with

me missing ....

（张智中　译）

首行的两个"异"字，复用以极写他乡之思；"独"、"客"二字，于此又有助益。九月九日重阳之"佳节"，诗人本该归乡，却因故而不能身归，因而"倍思亲"。译诗用 alone, lonely 和 strange, stranger 两组同源词语来译，正衬托诗人"独"在"异"乡之感慨。

"佳节"，英译 Height-Climbing Day 出之，以与随后之"登高"（at the height of the mountain）形成呼应，打通脉络。

"遥知兄弟登高处，遍插茱萸少一人。"英译：My mental picture: the cornel wearers at the height of the mountain are my brothers, with me missing ...　回译：

"我内心的图景——登上山顶的头戴茱萸者，是我的兄弟，只是少我一人……。"细而究之，"遥知"，英译变成了"内心的图景"，字面上似不忠实，却正是原诗之内在意蕴。所谓"遥知"，实乃"遥想"——既然诗人"独在异乡为异客"，家里"兄弟登高"之时，诗人只能心眼遥望，心中遥想了啊。那么，英译 my mental picture（我内心的图景），恰译其精神矣。

另外，译诗若散文读之：Alone, a lonely stranger in a strange land, on the Height-Climbing Day I turn my thoughts to my kinsfolk. My mental picture: the cornel wearers at the height of the mountain are my brothers, with me missing …诗意似未曾少减。采取自由诗行排列，则是向当代英诗靠拢的尝试和努力。

（96）赠别二首（二）（杜牧）

赠别二首（二）	Two Parting Poems (No. 2)
多情却似总无情， 唯觉樽前笑不成。 蜡烛有心还惜别， 替人垂泪到天明。	Affectionate, yet seemingly dispassionate; no smile is coaxed before a wine cup. The candle hates to say goodbye: it drops tears throughout the night. （张智中　译）

英文句子：

Constance **drank deeply** as Lady de Winter's **smile widened**. Suddenly, both women heard the pounding of hoofbeats.

看到康斯坦丝喝了一大口，德·温特夫人笑得更开心了。突然，两个女人都听到了马蹄声。

这里，drank deeply 和 smile widened，用语平白却十分有力。改译如下：

Two Parting Poems (No. 2)　Du Mu

Affectionate, yet seemingly dispassionate;

drinking deeply and heavily, no smile

is widened before a wine cup.

The candle hates to bid

adieu: it keeps weeping throughout

the night.

（张智中　译）

（97）清平调词三首（其一）（李白）

清平调词三首（其一） 云想衣裳花想容， 春风拂槛露花浓。 若非群玉山头见， 会向瑶台月下逢。	**Three Poems to Concubine Yang (1)** Clouds are her dress and flowers are her face; balustrade blown in spring breeze; flowers heavy with dewdrops. Such a rare beauty, if not seen in the immortal mountain, will be admired in the moonlit abode of fairies. （张智中　译）

后来读到这样的英文句子：

But **as chance would have it**, you did get into college…

谁知你偏偏就考上了……

这里，as chance would have it，"凑巧"之意。觉得可以借用，来改译"若非群玉山头见，会向瑶台月下逢"里面所暗含的语气。大体如此：As chance would have it, a rare beauty can be seen in the immortal mountain。改译如下：

Three Poems to Concubine Yang (1)

Clouds are her dress and flowers are her face;

balustrade blown in spring breeze; flowers

heavy with dewdrops. Such a rare beauty,

as chance would have it, if not seen

in the immortal mountain, will

be admired in the moonlit

abode of fairies.

（张智中　译）

这样一来，便觉得诗歌的语气，读起来好多了。

（98）东栏梨花——和孔密州五绝之一（苏轼）

英译宋代诗歌绝句时，非常喜欢苏轼的"人生看得几清明？"但其英译，却左右为难，难以尽妙。这里的"清明"，写的是一种人生态度：清明透彻，旷达超脱。正在为英文表达犯愁，正好读到这么一句英文：

Harold's **mind grew limpid**, and his body melted.

哈罗德的脑海渐渐澄明，身体像是融化了。

这里，名词 mind 与形容词 limpid 的搭配，正好表达了"清明"之人生态度。英译的难题，瞬间得以解决。

东栏梨花——和孔密州五绝之一　苏轼 梨花淡白柳深青， 柳絮飞时花满城。 惆怅东栏一株雪， 人生看得几清明？	**Pear Blossoms in My Courtyard　Su Shi** Pear blossoms are delicately white when willow twigs are deeply green; willow catkins are fanning, whirling, drifting, and wafting — filling the whole town. My heart, melancholy, is like the snow-white pear blossoms against the eastern balustrade in my courtyard, and my limpid mind is detached from the secular world of flashiness, noisiness, and transitoriness. （张智中　译）

（99）题都城南庄（崔护）

题都城南庄 去年今日此门中， 人面桃花相映红。 人面不知何处去， 桃花依旧笑春风。	**Written on the Wall of the Village** This day last year before this very door, a girl's face and peach flowers bloom against each other. But now where is the fair face of the girl? Only peach flowers are smiling in the spring breeze. （张智中　译）

读英文句子：

Her face turned **a delicate pink**.

她的脸微微发红，娇艳无比。

竟然把 pink 用作名词，前面用形容词 delicate 来修饰。这样的"人面"，正是崔护心中的"人面"。

又读到这样一个句子：

She was a plump girl **with a rosy bloom to her cheeks**.

似乎桃花飞到她的脸上。

改译如下：

Written on the Wall of the Village　Cui Hu

Last year this day before this very door,

a girl's face and peach flowers bloom

against each other. But now ——

where is the fair face, a delicate

pink, with a rosy bloom to her

cheeks? Only peach flowers

are giggling in the breeze

of the empty

spring.

（张智中　译）

改译中，除了 a delicate pink, with a rosy bloom to her cheeks 的添加之外，破折号的使用，强调了 now 与 last year 的今昔对比。另外，添加 empty 来修饰 spring，正写"人面不知何处去"之后，心里的失落感和空荡感。

又读英文名著《飘》（*Gone with the Wind*），见到几个句子：

A flush of embarrassment on Stuart's brown **cheeks**.

这时斯图尔特褐色的脸膛上泛起了一抹红晕。

The ladies were **pink with blushes**.

小姐太太们听得有点脸红了。

There was a tenseness about her, a glow in her eyes that he had never seen before, and even in the dim light he could see **the rosy flush on her cheeks**.

她浑身紧张，眼睛里闪烁着他从未见过的光辉，即使在阴暗中他也能看见她脸上泛着玫瑰似的红晕。

Why not take **this pretty, flushed boy**? He was as good as anyone else and she didn't care. No, she could never care about anything again, not if she lived to be ninety.

干吗不拿下这个脸蛋儿红仆仆的漂亮小伙子呢？他和旁的小伙

子一样，她也一样不感兴趣，不，她从此对任何事物也不会感兴趣了，哪怕活到 90 岁也罢。

There were **fresh roses in her sash that matched her cheeks**, and her cornflower-blue eyes were dancing with excitement.

她的饰带上佩着新鲜的玫瑰花，这同她的两颊相到辉映，那双矢车菊般的蓝眼睛更是兴奋得神采飞扬了。

The rose blushes in the morning breeze.

玫瑰花的脸在清晨的微风中泛红。

借鉴如上描写脸红的英文表达，《题都城南庄》可进一步改译。如果发挥英文诗行排列的优势，并适当调整一些字句，可得《题都城南庄》如下 4 种英译，并比较裘小龙和许渊冲的英译：

| **Written on the Wall of the Village**
Cui Hu
This day last year before this very door,
　a pretty girl is pink with blushes,
　　and her rosy flushed cheeks are
matched by fresh peach blossoms.
　But now where is the fair face
　　of the girl? Only peach
　　　petals are smiling
　　　　in the spring
　　　　　breeze.
　　　　（张智中　译） | **Written on the Wall of the Village**　Cui Hu
This day, last year, before
　this very door, peach blossoms
　　blush in the gentle breeze,
　　　against the blush of a pretty
　　　　girl. But now where is her
　　　　　fair face? — only peach

petals are beaming
　and smiling in
　　the spring breeze.
（张智中　译） |
| **Written on the Wall of the Village**
Cui Hu
This day, last year,
before this very door,
a pretty girl is pink with
blushes, and her rosy cheeks
are matched by fresh peach blossoms,
which bloom against
　　　　　each
other.
This day, this year — | **Written on the Wall of the Village**　Cui Hu
This day, last year, before
　this very door, peach blossoms
　　blush in the gentle breeze,
against the blush of a pretty
　girl. But now where is her
　　fair face? — only peach

petals are beaming
　and smiling in
　　the spring breeze.
（张智中　译） |

where is the fair face, a delicate pink, with a rosy bloom to her cheeks? Only peach flowers are giggling in the breeze 　　　　　　　of the empty 　　　　　　　　　spring. （张智中　译）	
Lines on South Village　Cui Hu This door, this day, last year, you blushed, the blushing faces of the peach blossoms reflecting yours. 　　This door, this day, this year, where are you, the peach blossoms still giggling at the spring breeze? （裘小龙　译）[81]	**Written in a Village South of the Capital** Cui Hu In this house on this day last year, a pink face vied In beauty with the pink peach blossoms side by side. I do not know today where the pink face has gone; In vernal breeze still smile pink peach blossoms full-blown. （许渊冲　译）[82]

　　裘小龙的译文，却在抛弃了原诗的形美之后，独辟蹊径，另有设计。特别是用 This door, this day, last year 与 This door, this day, this year 形成时间前后的对照与反衬，取得良好的效果。许渊冲的译文，以 4 行译 4 行，尾韵格局采取随韵：aabb，每行 12 个音节，可谓中规中矩。

（100）华子冈（王维）

华子冈 飞鸟去不穷， 连山复秋色。 上下华子冈， 惆怅情何极！	Huazi Mound The flight of birds never ends; autumn tints dye a hill after another hill. Up and down Huazi Mound, a sense of loss knows no bounds. （张智中　译）

---

81 裘小龙，汉英对照中国古典爱情诗词选［Z］，上海：上海社会科学院出版社，2003：31。

82 许渊冲，唐诗三百首：汉英对照［Z］，北京：海豚出版社，2013：154-155。

读英文：

She sighed often as if **a deep problem pressed itself against her**.

她常常叹气，好像有什么严重的问题压在她心头。

英语反身代词，构成英语语言的优势之一。如此妙用，汉语难传。而汉译英之时，若善加利用，则传原文微妙之情。改译如下：

Huazi Mound　Wang Wei

The flight of birds never ends; autumn

tints dye a hill after another hill.

Up and down Huazi Mound,

a sense of loss, pressing

itself against me,

knows no

bounds.

（张智中　译）

这样一来，惆怅之情或失落之感，便有了一种压迫感：抒写淋漓而尽致。

（101）绝句四首（三）（杜甫）

读英文，见到这样一个英文句子：

There was no way through it, and the front **windows** of the doctor's lodgings **commanded a pleasant little vista of** street that had a congenial air of retirement on it.

那儿没有街道穿过，从屋前的窗口望去，可以看到一片小小的风景，具有一种远离尘嚣的雅趣，令人心旷神怡。

描写窗户之景，command a pleasant little vista of，不正可用来英译"窗含西岭千秋雪"吗？没有读到这个句子之前，当然是不会这样英译的。

绝句四首（三）　杜甫	**Four Quatrains (No. 3)**　Du Fu
两个黄鹂鸣翠柳，	Two golden orioles twitter
一行白鹭上青天。	in emerald willow; a flock
窗含西岭千秋雪，	of white egrets fly heavenward.
门泊东吴万里船。	The window frames snow
	through thousands of years
	atop the West Ridge;

	the door sees ships from East China
	which have covered thousands of miles.
	（张智中　译）

改译：

Four Quatrains (No. 3)　Du Fu

The emerald willow is shivering with the twitters

of two golden orioles, when a flock of white

egrets are flying heavenward. The window

commands a pleasant little vista of snow

atop the West Ridge through thousands

of years, and the door sees ships

from East China, which have

covered thousands

of miles.

（张智中　译）

译诗如果散读，则是：

The emerald willow is shivering with the twitters of two golden orioles, when a flock of white egrets are flying heavenward. The window commands a pleasant little vista of snow atop the West Ridge through thousands of years, and the door sees ships from East China, which have covered thousands of miles.

其中，The window commands a pleasant little vista of snow atop the West Ridge through thousands of years，因为借用，自然是好的英文句子。

这样改译之后，又读到一些英文句子：

And **from every window there were beauties to be seen**.

从哪一个窗口望出去都美不胜收。

From its windows, the hill, upon which were many trees, was very beautiful.

从窗子望出去，那座小山，林木葱郁，是个十分美丽的地方。

显然，如果把这样的句子稍作改写，也可用来英译此一绝句。因此，再次改译如下，并回译汉语：

Four Quatrains (No. 3)　Du Fu	绝句四首（三）　杜甫
The emerald willow is shivering with the twitters of two golden orioles, when a flock of white egrets are flying heavenward. The window, from which there are beauties to be seen, commands a pleasant little vista atop the West Ridge, upon which is a blanket of snow through thousands of years, and the door sees ships from East China, which have covered thousands of miles. （张智中　译）	翠柳哆嗦着，由于两个黄鹂的啼鸣——当一行白鹭蓝天飞行。临窗远眺：美不胜收，框中小小的风景，茫茫西岭白雪——如斯千年，门前泊船，自东方，万里而来。 （张智中　译）

改译中，实际上添加了 from which there are beauties to be seen 和 upon which is a blanket of snow 两个短语，分别来源于上引的两个英文句子。这样的添加，当然是合理添加：是为了增进诗意的添加，而且不悖原意。

至于汉语回译，如果我们把这个译文当做今译，来和常见的其它今译相比的话，就会发现如此今译的一个显著特点：新诗化与现代化。翻译的手法，灵活而不拘泥，跳脱而不离题。如此翻译，才能走向译诗的成功。

如此英译，也算感觉比较满意。但是，后来又读到这样的英文句子：

The bar is in full swing, and floating rounds of cocktails permeate the garden outside, until **the air is alive with** chatter and laughter, ...

借用这个句子，英译杜甫此诗，我们似可这样来译：when the blue sky is alive with a flock of white egrets in flight，如此，乃是美丽英文。

She spoke in the soft slurring voice of the coastal Georgian, **liquid** of vowels, kind to consonants and with the barest trace of French accent.

她说话用的是海滨佐治亚人那种柔和而有点含糊的口音，元音是流音，子音咬得不怎么准，略微带法语腔调。

Their lazy, blurred **voices fell pleasantly on his ears**, but his own brisk brogue clung to his tongue.

他们那种懒洋洋的含糊不清的声音，他唱得特别悦耳，但他们自己那轻快的土腔却总是吊在舌头上摆脱不了。

借用如上英文，则杜甫《绝句四首（三）》又可英译如下，并比较许渊冲的英译：

Four Quatrains (No. 3) Du Fu The liquid voices of two orioles in emerald willows fall pleasantly on the ears, when the blue sky is alive with a flock of white egrets in flight. The window frames snow through thousands of years atop the West Ridge, and the door sees ships from East China which have covered thousands of miles. （张智中 译）	A Quatrain Du Fu Two golden orioles sing amid the willows green; A flock of white egrets flies into the blue sky. My window frames the snow-crowned western mountain scene; My door oft says to eastward-going ships "Goodbye!" （许渊冲 译）[83]

（102）夜看扬州市（王建）

唐代诗人王建描写扬州的诗及其英译：

夜看扬州市 王建 夜市千灯照碧云， 高楼红袖客纷纷。 如今不是时平日， 犹自笙歌彻晓闻。	Night View of the Fair of Yangzhou Wang Jian The night fair is bright with thousands of lamps lighting up clouds in the blue sky; the mansions are noisy with red-sleeved showgirls and pleasure-seeking visitors. Common days of peace no more, still snatches of singing and laughter are heard through the night. （张智中 译）[84]

笔者另有一个较为"繁琐"的译文：

Night View of the Fair of Yangzhou　Wang Jian

The night fair is fair with thousands of gay-colored

lamps, to light up clouds in the green sky; the high

tower is noisy with red sleeves and visitors

seeking pleasure. The usual days of joy

and peace no more: the nation swaying

in the midst of a raging storm; still

snatches of singing, laughter and

---

83 许渊冲，唐诗三百首：汉英对照［Z］，北京：海豚出版社，2013：97。
84 张智中，诗意扬州：汉英对照［Z］，北京：外语教学与研究出版社，2020：23。

reed piping — a great vibration

of voices throughout

the night.

（张智中　译）

译文中，gay-colored lamps 来自下面这个英文句子：

Music and singing were going on, and as the evening darkened hundreds of **gay-colored lamps** were lit.

音乐和歌声持续着，当夕阳余晖逐渐变得昏暗的时候，数以百计各式各样的灯就被点亮了起来。

译文最后三行的 still snatches of singing, laughter and reed piping — a great vibration of voices throughout the night，改写自下面英文句子：

The English visitors could hear the occasional twanging of a zither, the strumming of a piano, **snatches of laughter and shouting and singing, a faint vibration of voices**.

英国人听得到偶然传来的奇特琴声、漫不经心敲出来的钢琴声和说笑、喊叫及歌声，不过听不大清。

（103）鸟鸣涧（王维）

鸟鸣涧　王维 人闲桂花落， 夜静春山空。 月出惊山鸟， 时鸣春涧中。	**Birds Twittering Ravine**　Wang Wei People idle when osmanthus flowers fall, the night still and spring mountain empty. The moonrise startles the mountain birds, which once in a while twitter in spring ravine. （张智中　译）

后来，读到这样一个英文句子：

A silence took possession of the little room and, under cover of it, I approached the table and tasted my sherry and then returned quietly to my chair in the corner.

又见到 once in a while 添加定语的语法：**once in a great while**。

觉得 A silence took possession of the little room 这样的表达很好，正好可以用来表达"夜静春山空"之静谧状态；once in a great while 读来节奏感更好。于是改译如下：

Birds Twittering Ravine　Wang Wei

People idle and osmanthus flowers fall,

when a silence takes possession of

the empty spring mountain

enveloped in the night.

The moonrise startles

mountain birds

into twittering once

in a great while

in spring ravine.

（张智中　译）

另外，原译 The moonrise startles the mountain birds, which once in a while twitter in spring ravine，改为：The moonrise startles mountain birds into twittering once in a great while in spring ravine。首先，去掉 the mountain birds 中的定冠词；其次，用介词 into 与动词 startles 搭配，描写更加形象。

后来，又读到 deep peace 这样的搭配，觉得鲜活：

We listened intently, but nothing save the calling of the birds broke **the deep peace of** the forest.

我们仔细地听了听，周围一片寂静，只有小鸟打破树林间深沉的寂静。

下面两个句子：

He bore his misfortune with his habitual **tranquility**.

他以自己一贯的平静承受着这次不幸。

The rows of houses were **uniform** in appearance.

这一排排的房屋外表都是一样的。

觉得其中的形容词 uniform 和名词 tranquility 可以搭配，用 uniform tranquility 来描述"春山空"之时的"夜静"。

含有短语 break in on 的英文句子：

He opened the wrong door and **broke in on** a private conference.

他开错了门，闯入一间正在开私人会议的房间。

Don't **break in on** their conversation.

别打断他们的谈话。

Break in on one's thought.

突然想起。

王维诗中的"桂花"，似乎正可作为动词短语 break in on（upon）的主语；而"山鸟"，似乎可用作打破 deep peace 的主语。整首诗改译如下：

The Deep Peace of Spring Dale　Wang Wei

The falling of osmanthus flowers, witnessed by idlers,

is the only sound that breaks in upon the uniform

tranquility of the empty spring mountain

veiled in still night. The occasional

twittering of mountain birds,

startled by moonrise,

breaks the deep

peace of the

spring

dale.

（张智中　译）

王维《鸟鸣涧》，著名诗人洛夫的解构，极富诗意，是古诗经典当代化的一种重构。从翻译的角度观之，似乎不乏批评之音；但就独立的诗歌来看，却是难得的佳作。洛夫的唐诗解构之作，具独立之美学品格，见之大喜，起翻译之意矣。

刚拿起笔想写点什么	On the point of writing with penpoint
窗外的桂花香	A puff of scent from may flowers without the window
把灵感全熏跑了	
他闲闲地负手阶前	Has blown away his inspiration
这般月色，还有一些些，一点点……	Idly, his hands clasped behind his back before the steps
月亮从空山窜出	The moonlight, slightly moony, slightly dreamy …
吓得众鸟扑翅惊飞	

呱呱大叫 把春山中的空 把春涧中的静 全都吵醒 而他仍在等待 静静地 等待，及至 月，悄悄降落在稿纸上 让光填满每个空格 （洛夫）[85]	The moon leaps out of the empty mountain To startle a bevy of birds into flapping and fluttering While cawing and squawking Which awaken The emptiness of spring mountain The quietness of spring ravine And he is still waiting Quietly Waiting, until The moon, quietly descends on the draft paper For the light to fill each and every blank （张智中 译）

（104）早发白帝城（李白）

早发白帝城　李白 朝辞白帝彩云间， 千里江陵一日还。 两岸猿声啼不住， 轻舟已过万重山。	**Morning Departure from White King City**　Li Bai In the morning I leave White King City, crowned with clouds; in the same day I reach Jiangling, which is hundreds of miles away. The monkeys are crying along the banks, when my boat has passed through thousands of mountains. （张智中 译）

后来，读到三个相关的英文句子：

The two accidents happened **on the selfsame day**.

这两起意外事故发生在同一天。

The miles sped past, but she barely saw them.

一路飞驰，莫琳几乎没有留意窗外的景色。

He could **barely** get the words out.

他几乎连这句话都说不出来。

第一个句子的启发：原译 in the same day，若改为 on the selfsame day，则更加地道。第二个和第三个句子的启发：The miles sped past（很多英里飞逝而

---

85 洛夫，唐诗解构［M］，南京：江苏凤凰文艺出版社，2015：17-18。

去），既然目的地是"千里江陵"，速度又很快："轻舟已过万重山"，那么，似可改译：miles and miles speed past。

另外，第二个和第三个句子中的副词 barely，也感觉可用。原译 The monkeys are crying along the banks，改为：The crying of monkeys, all the way along the banks, is barely imperceptible by the ear。这样一来，译文由抽象变具象，由笼统变具体了。整首诗改译如下：

Morning Departure from White King City　Li Bai

The morning sees me taking leave of White King City,

which is crowned with clouds and, on the selfsame

day, I reach Jiangling, which is hundreds of

miles away. The crying of monkeys, all

the way along the banks, is barely

imperceptible by the ear, when

miles and miles speed past,

my boat passing through

thousands of

mountains.

（张智中　译）

除了上述改译之外，还把 In the morning I leave White King City, crowned with clouds，改为 The morning sees me taking leave of White King City, which is crowned with clouds and …。这样一来，不仅发挥了英文无灵主语的优势，语气也变得更加贯通。

（105）贾生（李商隐）

李商隐的讽刺诗《贾生》及其英译：

贾生　李商隐 宣室求贤访逐臣， 贾生才调更无伦。 可怜夜半虚前席， 不问苍生问鬼神。	**Jia Yi**　Li Shangyin Emperor Han Wendi is after talents, and he finds Jia Yi unparalleled. In Endless Joy Palace they talk at dead of night about ghosts stories instead of people's livelihood. （张智中　译）

译完此诗，我们又读到这样一个英文句子：

Words seemed to slip out of his mouth without noise, and she had **to crane her head closer in order to catch them**.

一句话就这样无声无息地从他一开一合的嘴唇里滑出来，莫琳要努力将身子探前去才能听到。

似乎是天意做巧，这句好真是极好地描写了《贾生》里汉文帝与贾谊两人深夜谈话的情景。改译如下：

Jia Yi   Li Shangyin

Emperor Han Wendi is after talents, and he finds

Jia Yi unparalleled, out of whose mouth words

seem to slip without noise at dead of night

in Endless Joy Palace, and the emperor

has to crane his head closer in order

to catch them. But they talk about

ghosts stories, instead of

people's livelihood.

（张智中　译）

又，读到菲茨杰拉德（Fitzgerald）《了不起的盖茨比》（*The Great Gatsby*）中的几个句子：

By midnight the hilarity had increased.

午夜时分，大家更有兴致了。

As our credulity switched back to her, she **leaned forward with enthusiasm**.

我们转而又信了她的话，她便又兴趣盎然地凑前说。

"Don't hurry, Meyer," said Gatsby, **without enthusiasm**.

"不要这么着急，迈耶。"盖茨比淡淡地说。

李商隐之《贾生》另译如下，并比较许渊冲的英译：

Jia Yi Li Shangyin	**A Bright Scholar** Li Shangyin
Emperor Han Wendi favors talents, and he finds Jia Yi unparalleled. In Endless Joy Palace, by midnight their interest	The emperor recalled the banished scholar bright, Peerless in eloquence and in ability. Alas! His Majesty drew near him at midnight

has not been decreased. Leaning forward with great enthusiasm, they talk at dead of night about ghosts stories instead of people's livelihood. （张智中　译）	To consult not on man but on divinity. （许渊冲　译）[86]

　　显然，许渊冲的英译与汉语诗歌在字面上比较吻合，而我们借鉴英文之后的英译，却更加明白清晰、达意顺畅。

（106）七绝·为女民兵题照（毛泽东）

　　这首诗，许渊冲的英译，颇有争议：

七绝·为女民兵题照　毛泽东 飒爽英姿五尺枪， 曙光初照演兵场。 中华儿女多奇志， 不爱红装爱武装。	**Militia Women — Inscription on a Photo** Mao Zedong So bright and brave, with rifles five feet long, At early dawn they shine on drilling place. Most Chinese daughters have desire so strong To face the powder, not powder the face. （许渊冲　译）[87]

　　这个译文中，争议最大的是最后一行"不爱红装爱武装"的英译：To face the powder, not powder the face。一些人，包括译者本人，非常得意，觉得是妙译，但也有人反对，觉得是文字游戏，甚至不知所云。

　　这个我们姑且不论，先看与此诗相关的一些句子。首先，霍克斯英译《红楼梦》第三回中的三个句子：

　　　　台阶上坐着几个穿红着绿的丫头。

　　Some gaily-dressed maids were sitting on the steps of the main building opposite.

　　　　及进入正室，早有许多艳妆丽服之姬妾丫鬟迎着。

　　Heavily made-up and expensively dressed maids and concubines,

---

86 许渊冲，唐诗三百首：汉英对照［Z］，北京：海豚出版社，2013：210。
87 许渊冲，精选毛泽东诗词与诗意画［Z］，北京：五洲传播出版社，2006：102。

who had been waiting in readiness, came forward to greet them.

越显得面如傅粉，唇若施脂，转盼多情，语言若笑。

She was even more struck than before by his fresh complexion. **The cheeks might have been brushed with powder** and the lips touched with rouge, so bright was their natural colour.

霍克斯英译《红楼梦》第七回中的三个句子：

薛姨妈道："姨太太不知，宝丫头怪着呢，他从来不爱这些花儿粉儿的。"

"You don't know our Bao-chai. She is funny about these things. She has **never liked ornaments or make-up or anything of that sort.**"

周瑞家的这才往贾母这边来，过了穿堂，顶头忽见他的女孩儿打扮着才从他婆家来。

Zhou Rui's wife now made her way towards Grandmother Jia's apartments. Just as she was coming out of the covered passage-way, she ran head-on into her daughter, all **dressed up in her best clothes** having just arrived on a visit from her mother-in-law's.

那秦钟见了宝玉，形容出众，举止不凡，更兼金冠绣服，艳婢娇童……

At the same time, Qin Zhong, struck by Bao-yu's **rare good looks** and princely beating and ── even mote perhaps ── by the golden coronet and **embroidered clothing** and the train of pretty maids and handsome pages who attended him …

另外两个类似的英文句子：

I do not wish to hear your clever speech on **the charms of the military**.

我不想听到你那有关军人魅力的精彩演讲。

Then he put away the letter, **a radiant glow washing over his face**.

收起情书，此时有光彩从脸上溢出。

显然，这些句子中，一些短语或表达与此诗密切相关，似可借用。我们来看西方译者的译文：

Inscription on a Photograph of Women Militia

These well-groomed heroines carry five-foot rifles,

On this parade ground in the first rays of the sun.

Daughters of China have uncommon aspirations,

Preferring battle-tunics to red dresses.

（Anne Fremantle 译）[88]

译文似乎没有对如上英文资源的利用。因此，译文显得平淡，只是散文化的释意而已。如果我们适当借用上引英文资源，可尝试英译《七绝·为女民兵题照》，散文如下：

These women, armed with five-footed rifles, are bathed in the first rays of the sun over the parade ground, a radiant glow washing over their faces, full of the charms of the military. Chinese daughters have high aspirations: preferably, they love military uniforms, instead of ornaments or embroidered clothing.

然后，整首诗诗体排列如下：

Inscription on the Photo of Militia Women　Mao Zedong

These women, armed with five-footed rifles, are bathed

in the first rays of the sun over the parade ground,

a radiant glow washing over their faces, full

of the charms of the military. Chinese

daughters have high aspirations:

preferably, they love military

uniforms, instead of

ornaments or

embroidered

clothing.

（张智中　译）

至少，从散文的角度而言，这是更好的散文表述。

---

88 Anne Fremantle, Mao Tse-tung: an Anthology of His Writings — Updated and Expanded to Include a Special Selection of the Poems of Mao, New York, New American Library Inc., 1972: 352.

（107）送元二使安西（王维）

| 送元二使安西　王维
渭城朝雨浥轻尘，
客舍青青柳色新。
劝君更尽一杯酒，
西出阳关无故人。 | **A Farewell Song**　Wang Wei
The morning rain of Weicheng settles the light dust and subdues
the dusty atmosphere, leaving the inn blue and the willows
fresh. Before the sun gains in strength, there is a clean
sweetness in the morning air, when we are
drinking and reveling in the freshness.
I urge you to drink, to drink another
cup of wine: beyond the Sunny
Pass, your westward journey
will find no good
friend like
me.
（张智中　译） |

英译若散文读之，则是：

The morning rain of Weicheng settles the light dust and subdues the dusty atmosphere, leaving the inn blue and the willows fresh. Before the sun gains in strength, there is a clean sweetness in the morning air, when we are drinking and reveling in the freshness. I urge you to drink, to drink another cup of wine: beyond the Sunny Pass, your westward journey will find no good friend like me.

品读可知，译文多处发挥了英文语言的优势。包括无灵主语的运用，如 The morning rain…settles 和 your westward journey will find …等；头韵的运用，如 dust 与 dusty，settles 与 subdues，find 与 friend 等；单词尾韵的运用，如 drinking 和 reveling 等；反复，如两用 to drink 等。

另外，译诗借鉴了 Miss Read 英文小说 *Tyler's Row* 中的两个句子：

Two days of heavy rain had left the countryside fresh and shining.

There was a clean sweetness in the morning air, as **the sun gained in strength**, and Diana turned down the window of the car, **revelling in the freshness.** How could one be despondent on such an exhilarating day? How could anything go wrong?

又，读到这样一个英文句子：

The road and **rooftops were bathed in softest blue**.

所有屋顶、马路都浸在一片最柔软的蓝色里。

正可用来英译"渭城朝雨浥轻尘"之后的景色："客舍青青柳色新"。于是，《送元二使安西》又有新译，并比较许渊冲的译文：

A Farewell Song　Wang Wei	**A Farewell Song**　Wang Wei
After the morning rain of Weicheng settles the dust, rooftops of the inns are bathed in softest blue, over which fresh willows are waving lingeringly. I urge you to drink, to drink another cup of wine: beyond the Sunny Pass, your west-ward journey will find no bosom friend like me.　（张智中　译）	No dust is raised on the road wet with morning rain; The willows by the hotel look so fresh and green. I invite you to drink a cup of wine again; West of the Sunny Pass no more friends will be seen. （许渊冲　译）[89]

如果从散文的角度来读，笔者的译文是：

> After the morning rain of Weicheng settles the dust, rooftops of the inns are bathed in softest blue, over which fresh willows are waving lingeringly. I urge you to drink, to drink another cup of wine: beyond the Sunny Pass, your westward journey will find no bosom friend like me.

读起来就像英文散文，但却颇堪玩味。许渊冲的译诗散读：

> No dust is raised on the road wet with morning rain; the willows by the hotel look so fresh and green. I invite you to drink a cup of wine again; west of the Sunny Pass no more friends will be seen.

比较之下，语言和内涵似乎显得单薄寡味。

---

89 许渊冲，唐诗三百首：汉英对照［Z］，北京：海豚出版社，2013：44。

（108）牧童诗（黄庭坚）

牧童诗　黄庭坚 骑牛远远过前村， 短笛横吹隔陇闻。 多少长安名利客， 机关用尽不如君。	**The Cowboy: a Gainer of Life**　Huang Tingjian The cowboy sits on an ox, passing by a distant mountain village, slowly and leisurely, while producing random tunes from his flute: audible across the fields. In the capital how many seekers of fame and gains: seeking, searching, and pursuing here and there, high and low, eventually are losers, instead of gainers. （张智中　译）

译诗散读：

> The cowboy sits on an ox, passing by a distant mountain village, slowly and leisurely, while producing random tunes from his flute: audible across the fields. In the capital how many seekers of fame and gains: seeking, searching, and pursuing here and there, high and low, eventually are losers, instead of gainers.

显然，英文语言的优势，又有发挥。例如 slowly 和 leisurely，形成单词尾韵；from，flute，fields，形成头韵；seeking，searching，pursuing 形成单词尾韵，同时 seeking 与 searching 又形成头韵；here and there 与 high and low，形成平行结构；最重要的，或许是三个 -er 后缀词的运用：seekers（追名逐利者），losers（失败者，人生的输家）和 gainers（人生的赢家）。在英语里，-er 后缀类词构成英文的优势之一。如此运用，常致译文韵味醇厚。

（109）游子吟（孟郊）

有时，读到英文句子中的一个表达，便会想到一首古诗的英译，并且不是古诗文字的表面，而是其深层含义里所具有的东西。例如下面这两个句子：

> The family's respect for tradition was, however, **a source of** great unease **to** him.

> The body that had been **a source of** endless warmth **to** him was now veiled by her touchy susceptibility.

> As a result, many people avoid the very attempts that are **the source**

of true happiness.

这三个句子中，a/the source of ... to ...的表达，婉转而可爱。想起孟郊的《游子吟》及其英译：

游子吟　孟郊	**Song of the Parting Son**　Meng Jiao
慈母手中线，	From the threads a mother's hand weaves
游子身上衣。	A gown for parting son is made,
临行密密缝，	Sewn stitch by stitch before he leaves
意恐迟迟归。	For fear his return be delayed,
谁言寸草心，	Such kindness as young grass receives
报得三春晖。	From the warm sun can be repaid?
	（许渊冲　译）[90]

上引英译，如果散读，则是：

From the threads a mother's hand weaves a gown for parting son is made, sewn stitch by stitch before he leaves for fear his return be delayed, such kindness as young grass receives from the warm sun can be repaid?

反复品读，总觉语言平淡。不仅如此，似乎还有问题：a mother's hand 做主语，与谓语动词 weaves 搭配，自然吗？接下来，weaves a gown for parting son is made，似乎不太通顺。

好了，如果我们利用 a source of great unease to ...，可尝试英译，先散文英译如下：

The busy thread in an affectionate mother's hands, over the clothes of a wanderer to keep warmth. Sewing stitch by stitch after stitch, before his parting, a source of great worry and unease to Mother, afraid her son will return home late. The heart of an inch of grass — can it repay the favor and affection of sunshine in spring?

（张智中　译）

这样就通顺多了，而且，a source of great worry and unease to Mother，显然成为译文的语言亮点。诗行排列，则译诗如下：

Song of a Parting Son　Meng Jiao

The busy thread in an affectionate mother's hands,

---

90 许渊冲，唐诗三百首：汉英对照［Z］，北京：海豚出版社，2013：116。

over the clothes of a wanderer to keep warmth.

Sewing stitch by stitch after stitch, before his

parting, a source of great worry and unease

to Mother, afraid her son will return

home late. The heart of an inch

of grass —— can it repay

the favor and affection

of sunshine in

spring?

（张智中　译）

（110）牵牛花（陈宗远）

牵牛花　陈宗远 绿蔓如藤不用栽， 淡青花绕竹篱开。 披衣向晓还堪爱， 忽见蜻蜓带露来。	**The Morning Glory**　Chen Zongyuan Green vines creep into an overgrowth of tendrils without gardening; frail flowers, of a variety of pale colors, bloom into trumpets against the bamboo fence. Loveable is the morning glory when the early morning finds me admiring the flower with my clothes thrown on, which is graced by a dewy dragon- fly flying and flitting, and alighting. （张智中　译）

本来，译完此诗，感觉还比较满意。但后来又读到下面三个英文句子：

Her bamboo stakes **tilted at a drunken angle towards the ground,** and the tips of her bean plants **groped their blind passage into air.**

她花园里的竹架子像喝醉酒一样弯向地面，种下的豆藤只能摸索着向空中伸展。

Their front gardens, however, sloped at a precarious angle towards the pavement below, and plants **wrapped themselves round bamboo stakes as if hanging on for dear life.**

家家户户的花园都颤巍巍地向低处的马路倾斜，园里的植物都保命似的紧紧缠绕着竹栅栏。

The trees **gave up their branches to the wind as fluidly as**

tentacles in water.

　　树木终于放开了手，任枝叶像柔软的触角一样在风雨中推来搡去。

　　这三个句子中，对于花木的描写，形象而传神，而且描写的正好也是"绿蔓如藤"之状。

　　借用之后，《牵牛花》改译如下：

The Morning Glory　Chen Zongyuan

Green vines creep into an overgrowth of tendrils without gardening,

some tilting at a drunken angle towards the ground, and some

groping their blind passage into air; frail flowers, of a variety

of pale colors, bloom into trumpets against the bamboo

fence, wrapping themselves round it as if hanging on

for dear life, and giving up their tendrils to the wind

as fluidly as tentacles in water. Loveable is the

morning glory when the early morning finds

me admiring the flower with my clothes

thrown on, which is graced by a dewy

dragonfly flying and flitting,

and alighting.

（张智中　译）

（111）鹿柴（王维）

鹿柴　王维	**The Deer Park**　Wang Wei
空山不见人，	Empty hill: nobody is seen;
但闻人语响。	But human voice is echoing.
返景入深林，	Sunlight is reflected deep into the woods,
复照青苔上。	Where it alights on green moss aground. （张智中　译）

　　晨读英文，读到如下与《鹿柴》相关的英文句子：

　　…where **a wandering shaft of light fell full upon** the golden allamanda, ….

　　不经意的一束阳光洒落在金黄色的黄蔓……。

While Wolfert kept the light of the lanthorn turned **full upon it**, and watched it with the most breathless interest.

与此同时，沃尔弗特把提灯拧到最亮来照着魔杖，然后兴致勃勃、屏息凝神地注视着它。

The sun **beat full upon** them.

强烈的阳光照在他们身上。

The light of the street, no longer dimmed by the dusty glass, **fell full upon** his face.

街上的灯光不再受灰尘仆仆的玻璃遮挡，把他那张脸照得清清楚楚。

Holmes held up the paper so that **the sunlight shone full upon** it.

福尔摩斯把那张纸举起来，让阳光充分照亮它。

It is midnight; the breeze blows fairly, and the watch on deck scarcely stir. Again **there is a sound as of a human voice**, but hoarser.

现在已经是半夜了，微风习习，甲板上瞭望的水手也不爱动弹了。好像有人的声音传来，只是更沙哑些。

But in the forest the wind blew free, and the sunlight with **wandering** hands of gold moved the tremulous leaves aside.

然而在森林里，风儿自由自在地吹着，树叶随风摇曳，阳光透过树叶的缝隙照射过来，仿佛给它们镀上了一层金。

The wall can optimally absorb **the echoing sound**.

这墙能极有效地吸收回声。

Above, through **lacing boughs**, could be seen the stars.

上面，透过密密麻麻的树枝，可以看到星星。

She watched the sun **flickering down** through the warm-trunked redwoods.

她看着太阳光忽隐忽现地从长着温暖树干的红木树林中照射下来。

It was a summer camp of city-tired people, pitched in a grove of towering redwoods **through whose lofty boughs the sunshine trickled down, broken and subdued to soft light** and cool shadow.

这是一个由厌倦了城市生活的人组成的夏令营，搭建在长着参天红杉树的林子里，阳光从高高的枝条间隙里渗下来，经过树枝的阻挡阳光已变柔和，形成了阴凉的树阴。

借鉴如上英文表达，改译《鹿柴》三种如下：

The Deer Park　Wang Wei

The empty hill sees no soul;

yet human voice is echoing.

A wandering shaft of light,

through the deep woods,

fell full upon

the green moss

aground.

（张智中　译）[91]

The Deer Park　Wang Wei

The empty mountain sees

no soul, when some

whispering is echoing,

the sound as of a human

voice. A wandering shaft

of light, aslant through the

deep woods, falls full upon

the green moss aground.

（张智中　译）

A Secluded Forest Scene　Wang Wei

Not a single soul is seen

in the empty mountain —

save some whispering,

the echoing sound as of

a human voice — where

---

91 张智中，唐诗绝句英译 800 首：中英对照 [Z]，武汉：武汉大学出版社，2019：42。

　　　　　　　a wandering shaft of light,

　　　through lacing boughs of

　　　　　the forest, is flickering and

　　　　　　trickling down, broken and

　　　subdued to soft light,

　　　　　before falling full upon

　　　　　　the green moss aground.

　　　　　（张智中　译）

（112）过松源晨炊漆公店（杨万里）

过松源晨炊漆公店　杨万里	Passing by Songyuan　Yang Wanli
莫言下岭便无难， 赚得行人错喜欢。 正入万山圈子里， 一山放出一山拦。	Don't say downhill no obstacles before you lie, Misleading wayfarers to be happy and gay! You are surrounded by ten thousand mountains high: One mountain lets you pass, another bars your way.[92] （许渊冲　译）

　　译诗押交叉韵，每行 12 个音节，可谓工整。但是，从英语诗歌的角度来看，译诗还是缺少了点"英文气"。译文若没有"英文气"，西方读者就不会非常喜欢。正如英诗汉译，如果译诗缺乏汉语的气息，中国读者也不会喜欢，是一样的道理。在坚持每天阅读英文的情况下，我们尝试给出如下英译：

Illusive Relief in Mountain Walking　Yang Wanli

Downhill is not to be down with hard walking;

　mountaineers tend to be happy when illusively

　　relieved at the seemingly cheerful sight.

　In the mountain of mountains, one

　　peak topped, another unclimbed

　　gleaming white peak towers

　　　above all the

　　　others.

　　　　　（张智中　译）

　　首先，诗歌标题《过松源晨炊漆公店》，许渊冲简化为 *Passing by Songyuan*,

---

92 许渊冲，宋元明清诗选：汉英对照［Z］，北京：海豚出版社，2013：79。

我们觉得不太具有诗意。采用 *Illusive Relief in Mountain Walking*，其中，Illusive Relief 与诗行中的 illusively relieved 相呼应; Mountain Walking 与诗行中的 hard walking 相呼应。标题回译:《错喜欢: 山行中的错觉》，这就比直译标题来得更加巧妙。

译诗首行中，Downhill 与 down 形成同源词语，具修辞效果。另外，be down with 意为"打倒，不要; 放下，扔下"。这样搭配，诗行便有了新鲜感，有了值得玩味的余地和空间。

"行人"，英译采用 mountaineers（登山者），可暗喻人生如同登山，变通而佳。"错喜欢"，对应英文: tend to be happy when illusively relieved at the seemingly cheerful sight，英文地道，如同英文写作。这应该是翻译的最佳状态。

接下来，"正入万山圈子里，一山放出一山拦。"英译: In the mountain of mountains, one peak topped, another unclimbed gleaming white peak towers above all the others（在群山之中，登上一个山顶，却发现另一个山顶，白光闪烁，呈顶峰中的顶峰，未曾有人攀登。）

这里的英译，借鉴了好几个英文句子或短语:

He was the first **to top the mountain peak**.

The most difficult and the most beautiful **unclimbed peak** in the world.

Those **gleaming white peaks**.

This peak **towers above all the others**.

因此，译文耐读耐品。整首诗回译如下:

错喜欢: 山行中的错觉　　杨万里

下了一道岭，别以为行路，就不再难;

错以为如释重负，行人错喜欢——

面对看似令人快慰的坦途。在这

群山之中，爬上一个山中山，

却发现，另一个巍巍高山，

耸立远方，待登攀，

白光，烁烁

闪。

（张智中　译）

这样，杨万里终于得到了当代语境下的当代阐释。正是：如果杨万里活在当下，他该写出这样的当代诗歌的吧。

（113）上元夜（六首之一）（崔液）

有时，读到一个英文句子，便会觉得眼前一亮。例如：

The streets were thronged with ragged fellows ....

大街上拥挤着一群群衣衫褴褛的家伙。

就想起曾经的一首译诗：

上元夜（六首之一） 崔液	The Lantern Festival (No. 1 of six poems) Cui Ye
玉漏铜壶且莫催， 铁关金锁彻明开。 谁家见月能闲坐， 何处闻灯不看来！	Be slow of timing, clepsydra and copper kettle; the city gate will be open throughout the night. At the sight of the bright moon, who can sit idle? Lanterns high and low, the streets are thronged with watchers. （张智中 译）

最后一句的译文：the streets are thronged with watchers，是自己早先大胆使用的英文，后来读到英文里面地道的用法，得以印证，不觉令人兴奋。不过，经过一段时间的英文阅读，再看以前的译文，总感觉还可以润色提高：

The Lantern Festival (No. 1 of six poems) Cui Ye

Be slow of timing, clepsydra and copper kettle;

the city gate keeps open throughout the night.

The bright moon casts brilliant beams from

roof to roof, coupled with lanterns low

and high: the streets are thronged

with watchers — nobody

is a homebody.

（张智中 译）

添加的 coupled with，语言地道；nobody 与 homebody（喜欢待在家里的人）构成同源修辞格，并具幽默之效果。改译显然有所进步。

（114）十一月四日风雨大作（陆游）

有时，我们也可以从译文当中汲取语言营养，尤其是西方译者的译文。例如英国翻译家 Cranmer-Byng 对李白《静夜思》的英译：

Thoughts in a Tranquil Night

Athwart the bed

I watch the moonbeams cast a trail

So bright, so cold, so frail,

That for a space it gleams

Like hoar-frost on the margin of my dreams.

I raise my head, —

The splendid moon I see:

Then droop my head,

And sink to dreams of thee —

My fatherland, of thee!

（L. Cranmer-Byng　译）[93]

第五行译文，on the margin of my dreams（在我梦的边缘），很有诗意，可借用来英译其他古诗。例如陆游这首名诗：

十一月四日风雨大作　　陆游	**Composed in a Rainstorm**　Lu You
僵卧孤村不自哀， 尚思为国戍轮台。 夜阑卧听风吹雨， 铁马冰河入梦来。	Lying prostrate in a lonely bed, I am not self-pitied, still yearning to garrison the frontiers of my motherland. At dead of night I lend an ear to the stormy wind and rain; armored horses and icebound rivers enter my dream. （张智中　译）

翻译完，过了一段时间之后，对译文不太满意。借鉴如上 on the margin of my dreams，改译如下：

Composed in a Rainstorm　Lu You

Bedridden in a lonely bed, I cherish no self pity,

yearning to garrison frontiers of my mother-

land. At dead of night I lend an ear to

the stormy wind caught in rain,

---

before the sound of armored

horse hooves coming up

icebound rivers travels

to the margin of

my dream.

（张智中　译）

将"铁马冰河入梦来"英译为 the sound of armored horse hooves coming up icebound rivers travels to the margin of my dream（马的铁蹄之声沿着冰封的河流，一直流到我的梦之边缘）。

另外，这句英译还借鉴了如下英文：

She never heard **the sound of hooves coming up the river road** from Twelve Oaks that for a sweet moment she did not think—Ashley!

她只要听见马蹄声在那条从"十二橡树"村过来的河边大道上一路得得而至，便没有一次不想起艾希礼的！

这样，译诗便具有了当代诗的质感，诗意大增。

（115）和梅圣俞杏花（欧阳修）

和梅圣俞杏花　欧阳修 谁道梅花早？ 残年岂是春！ 何如艳风日， 独自占芳辰。	**In Reply to Mei Yaochen About Apricot Flowers** Ouyang Xiu Who says plum blossoms are the first bloomer? The dusk of the year falls short of a new spring. Unparalleled: in fine days of genial sunshine, apricot flowers, amidst a hundred of flowers, are uniquely eye-catching. （张智中　译）

后来，读 Black 英译沈复的《浮生六记》，其中有这么一句：

… each flower and tree seems to be trying to outshine the rest in brilliance and beauty.

觉得正好适合此诗的英译，于是改译如下：

In Reply to Mei Yaochen About Apricot Flowers　Ouyang Xiu

Who says plum blossoms are the first bloomer?

The dusk of the year falls short of a new

spring. In fine days of genial sunshine,

each flower and tree seems to be

trying to outshine the rest in

brilliance and beauty, when

apricot flowers are

particularly eye-

catching.

（张智中　译）

（116）鹊桥仙（秦观）

鹊桥仙　秦观 纤云弄巧， 飞星传恨， 银汉迢迢暗度。 金风玉露一相逢， 便胜却、人间无数。 柔情似水， 佳期如梦， 忍顾鹊桥归路。 两情若是久长时， 又岂在、朝朝暮暮。	**Immortals at Magpie Bridge**　Qin Guan The changing of flimsy clouds is irregular and artful; the shooting stars are pouring out their missing and yearning. Stealthily across the Silver River the Cowherd meets the Weaving Girl. A single annual meeting in the seventh evening of the seventh month amidst golden autumn wind & jade-glistening dew puts to shame countless couples in the mortal world. Water-like tender feelings, dreamy ecstatic tryst, at parting how can they bear to look back at the Magpie Bridge? So long as two sweet hearts are forever fondly in love, why in the company of each other from sweet morning to sweet evening and from sweet evening to sweet morning? （张智中　译）

译文采取典型的散文语言，来表达原诗的诗意内容。译文不追求译文与原文形式上的对应，只求采用地道的英文语言，来抒发诗人秦观之诗情。语言虽然力求归化，文化内容却尽力异化。例如，"银汉"或"银河"，英译没有采用英文里的已有表达 the Milky Way，而是直译出之：the Silver River；牛郎与织女，也分别照直意译：Cowherd 和 the Weaving Girl，以传达汉诗所包含之汉语文化因素。

英译中，flimsy clouds，puts to shame，ecstatic tryst，fondly in love，in the company of each other 等，都是地道之英文。"朝朝暮暮"的英译：from sweet morning to sweet evening and from sweet evening to sweet morning，在符合英文表达的前提下，有了译者的创造性使用。

（117）旅夜书怀（杜甫）

旅夜书怀　杜甫	**Night Sailing**　Du Fu
细草微风岸， 危樯独夜舟。 星垂平野阔， 月涌大江流。 名岂文章著， 官应老病休。 飘飘何所似？ 天地一沙鸥。	Riverside tender grass is dancing 　　gently under a breeze; a lonely tall mast is nosing through a vast 　　sheet of darkness. A maze of stars drooping over boundlessly 　　desolate field, the moon is surging and swinging as the 　　great river is swelling and undulating. The fame of a person 　　is established only from his literary pieces? An official, pestered by 　　sickness and old age, resigns from his post. Flapping, fluttering, floating, 　　what I am? Between heaven and earth, I am belittled to a mere wild gull, 　　wheeling in the boundless emptiness. （张智中　译）

原诗八行，译诗十六行，汉语一行，大体对应英译两行，这也是古诗英译常见的一种格局。译诗有多处英文借鉴。译文 a lonely tall mast is nosing through a vast sheet of darkness 中，动词 nose 大意："（车辆、船只等）缓慢地前行；（动物用鼻子）拱，嗅；勉强领先（或获胜）。"例如：

People kept **nosing around** the place, interrupting my work.

人们在这周围不断查看着，打断了我的工作。

短语 a vast sheet of 较为少见，但却生动形象。例如：

Vivid flashes of lightning dazzled my eyes, illuminating the lake, making it appear like **a vast sheet of** fire.

耀眼的闪电让我目眩，闪电照亮了湖水，使它看上去像是一片火海。

接下来，译文 A maze of stars drooping over boundlessly desolate field，借鉴如下两个英文句子：

The building is **a maze of** corridors.

这座建筑长廊交错，简直就是一座迷宫。

其中，名词 maze，表示"迷宫；错综复杂的事物；纵横交错的小街（或小道等）；迷惑"等意。

The branches of the **drooping** willows were swaying lightly.

垂柳轻飘飘地摆动。

随后的译文中，an official，名词，官员之意。例如：

An official pushed through the throng.

一位官员从人群中挤过。

动词 pester，表示"纠缠，烦扰；使烦恼"之意。例如：

People pester me and they **pester** others with inquiries about what I am doing.

人们不断打扰我，也互相打扰，打听我正在做什么。

"官应老病休"的英译，借鉴下句英文：

He **resigned from his post** as treasurer.

他辞去了司库的职务。

"天地一沙鸥"的英译：I am belittled to a mere wild gull, wheeling in the boundless emptiness，动词 wheel，表示"旋转，回旋"之意。例如：

Round and round her swam the dolphins, and **the wild gulls wheeled** above her head.

海豚便在她的周围游来游去，野海鸥也在她头顶上空盘旋。

I am belittled to a mere wild gull 则借鉴自当代英文诗歌。Rupi Kaur 的诗

集 Milk and Honey（Andrews McMeel Publishing 2015 年出版），其中有这么一句：

> One second they are holding you like the world in their lap and the next **they have belittled you to a mere picture**.

这里是主动语态，借鉴后的译文中，使用了被动语态，以便更好地再现杜甫诗歌之情韵。比较下面译文：

Mooring at Night　Du Fu

Riverside grass caressed by wind so light,

A lonely mast seems to pierce lonely night.

The boundless plain fringed with stars hanging low,

The moon surges with the river on the flow

Will fame ever come to a man of letters

Old, ill, retired, no official life betters?

What do I look like, drifting on so free?

A wild gull seeking shelter on the sea.

（许渊冲　译）[94]

译文语言借鉴英文之处，似不多见，译文显得平淡，尤其后四行的译文。译文如果能借鉴英文中好的表达，并善于变通，译诗往往更富意象，更有意境。

（118）望月怀远（张九龄）

读到下面两个英文句子：

> The moon cast her **mellow** light on the lake.

柔和的月光射在湖面上。

> The path of the righteous is like the first gleam of dawn, shining ever brighter till **the full light** of day.

但义人的路，好像黎明的光，越照越明，直到日午。

这里，英文单词 light 的前置定语 mellow 和 full，觉得破堪玩味。想起张九龄《望月怀远》中的"灭烛怜光满"，写明月之光，何其温情柔曼！而其英译，往往不太给力。若将 mellow 与 full 并用，修饰月光，似乎恰好。又读到

---

94 许渊冲，唐诗三百首：汉英对照［Z］，北京：海豚出版社，2013：97。

英文句子：

How could I have stayed **abed**!

我怎么能赖床呢！

副词 abed，似有文气逸出，可用。于是，得此诗英译如下：

望月怀远　张九龄	**Gazing at the Moon and Yearning Afar**　Zhang Jiuling
海上生明月， 天涯共此时。 情人怨遥夜， 竟夕起相思。 灭烛怜光满， 披衣觉露滋。 不堪盈手赠， 还寝梦佳期。	Over the sea a bright moon is born; the horizon shares the same moment. Lovers are afflicted by long night, throughout which they are yearning. Candle snuffed: mellow, full light; my coat feels the cold wetting dew. Moonbeams no gift by my hand, I go abed for a fond dream of you. （张智中　译）

比较另外二译：

Viewing the Moon and Thinking of the Dear One Afar　Zhang Jiuling	**Looking at the Moon and Longing for One Far Away**　Zhang Jiuling
Over the vast sea is rising up the moon bright. It shines on you afar and me this same instant. As a lover complaining of the long, long night, I sit up all the time, lovesick and in torment. I blow out the candle to see the moon's full light; I feel the cold wet dew and throw on my garment. Since to you I cannot make a gift of moonlight, I go to bed to dream of our meeting moment. （王玉书　译）[95]	Over the sea grows the moon bright; We gaze on it far, far apart. Lovers complain of long, long night; They rise and long for the clear heart. Candles blown out, fuller is light; My coat put on, I'm moist with dew. As I can't hand you moonbeams white, I go to bed to dream of you. （许渊冲　译）[96]

描写月光之美，两个译文都用了 full，很好，但 mellow 更可传月光柔和之神。表示"还寝梦佳期"之动作，两个译文都用了 I go to bed，而我们借用英文后的译文：I go abed for a fond dream of you，不仅多了一丝文气，for 与 fond 押头韵，abed 与 fond 押尾韵，节奏感更强一些。

95　王玉书．精选唐诗与唐画（汉英对照）[Z]．北京：五洲传播出版社，2005：46。
96　许渊冲．唐诗三百首：汉英对照 [Z]．北京：海豚出版社，2013：24。

（119）锦瑟（李商隐）

锦瑟　李商隐	**Golden Zither**　　Li Shangyin
锦瑟无端五十弦， 一弦一柱思华年。 庄生晓梦迷蝴蝶， 望帝春心托杜鹃。 沧海月明珠有泪， 蓝田日暖玉生烟。 此情可待成追忆， 只是当时已惘然。	Out of the fifty strings of the golden zither 　　musical notes are produced; each and every string reminiscent of the vanished springs 　　of my life. In his morning dream Zhuang Zi is transformed into a butterfly: he into a 　　butterfly or a butterfly into himself? The overthrown emperor, sorrow-stricken, dies 　　to be reincarnated into a cuckoo-bird who, with his blood-dripping beak, is twittering 　　plaintively in late spring. In the boundless sea brilliant under the bright wheel of moon, 　　countless glittering pearls are like teardrops of the legendary mermaid; the beautiful jade, 　　hidden deep in the Blue Mountain, gives off dim mist under the genial sun. This sight, this 　　scene, is sure to be a fond memory cherished in the depths of my heart — a pity, I, lacking 　　a sense of romance, have let slip a golden chance! （张智中　译）

译文中，"锦瑟"，用 golden zither，暗示金色年华；"只是当时已惘然"的英译，又用 a golden chance，强调了金色年华、黄金机遇之易逝。锦瑟之音，用 musical notes（音符），正好。例如：

Mozart actually learned how to write **musical notes** before he learned how to write words.

事实上，莫扎特在学会写字之前就学会如何写音符。

译诗中另有不少英文借用：

The way he laughed was strongly **reminiscent of** his father.

他笑的样子让人很容易想起他的父亲。

A **brilliant** sun lit up their rooms.

灿烂的阳光照亮了他们的屋子。

Dim smoke and **mist** have gone far with world affairs like dream.

飘渺的烟雾载着云梦般的世事远去。

They raced for the creek, a good many *mu* in extent, where as far as eye could see massed lotus leaves reached towards the **genial sun** like a solid wall of bronze.

她们奔着那不知道有几亩大小的荷花淀去，那一望无边际的密密层层的大荷叶，迎着阳光舒展开，就像铜墙铁壁一样。

A true friend will always extend a helping hand to you when you are **in the depths of** despair.

当你处于绝望的深渊时，真正的朋友总会伸出援助之手。

（120）酬耿少府见寄（戴叔伦）

酬耿少府见寄 戴叔伦 方丈萧萧落叶中， 暮天深巷起悲风。 流年不尽人自老， 外事无端心已空。 家近小山当海畔， 身留环卫荫墙东。 遥闻相访频逢雪， 一醉寒宵谁与同。	**To My Governor-Friend Through Falling Leaves** Dai Shulun As a monk I am fenced in a small room which fails to be fenced off from falling leaves, when a deep lane under the dusk sky is somber with a sorrowful wind. The years are running endlessly when I decline into the vale of years; my care-laden heart is utterly drained of solicitude by a chain of external events. You are to live in seclusion: in a hill by the sea, before resigning from your official post. Remote news: your intention to visit me is nipped by a heavy snowfall from time to time — when, in a cold night, can we get together to drink ourselves drunk? （张智中　译）

译诗中，有多处英文借鉴，主要如下：

The warm sunshine, **through the dense leaves falling down**, little golden spots.

和煦的阳光，透过稠密的树叶洒落下来，成了点点金色的光斑。

My room was so small that I felt **fenced in**.

我的房间很小，使我有困居斗室之感。

She felt **fenced in** by domestic routine.

她觉得自己完全被家务事束缚住了。

One end of the garden was **fenced off** for chickens.

花园的一端已用篱笆隔开来养鸡。

It is not manly for you to **fence off** the consequences of your action.

你要是回避你的行动后果，就不像个男子汉。

She looked up staring at the **somber** December sky.

她抬起头来，凝望着十二月份阴沉沉的天空。

I am **declining into the vale of years**.

我已入耄耋之年。

His voice **was utterly drained of** emotion.

他的声音再没有任何感情。

His future is my greatest **solicitude**.

他的前途是我最关心的问题。

They **live by the sea**.

他们住在海边。

A chilly reception **nipped** the first enthusiasm.

起初的满腔热忱遭到冷遇之后就消失了。

They **get together** once a year at Christmas time.

他们每年圣诞节时聚会一次。

He **has drunk himself sick**.

他喝酒太多，病倒了。

整首译诗，散读如下：

As a monk I am fenced in a small room which fails to be fenced off from falling leaves, when a deep lane under the dusk sky is somber with a sorrowful wind. The years are running endlessly when I decline into the vale of years; my care-laden heart is utterly drained of solicitude by a chain of external events. You are to live in seclusion: in a hill by the sea, before resigning from your official post. Remote news: your intention to visit me is nipped by a heavy snowfall from time to time — when, in a cold night, can we get together to drink ourselves drunk?

译诗首先必须是流畅且具美感的散文，才有可能是好的译诗，若连散文的标准都达不到，韵脚安排得再好，也是徒劳无益之功。

（121）绝句（志南）

偶然读到这样一个句子：

I feel touching my face **a tinge of warmth** from an unseen light.

我感觉迎面拂来一丝不知发自什么光体的暖意。

其中，a tinge of warmth 令人想起古诗名句"吹面不寒杨柳风"。又：

Harold sat **in a pocket of shade** and briefly watched the copper statue.

哈德罗在一片小阴影中坐了下来，看了一眼铜像。

I'll **walk you to** the bus stop.

我陪你走到汽车站。

这里，walk 是及物动词，比较少见，但却形象生动，表示"使走；陪……走；帮助……走"之意。综合借鉴之后，译诗如下：

绝句　志南 古木阴中系短篷， 杖藜扶我过桥东。 沾衣欲湿杏花雨， 吹面不寒杨柳风。	**A Quatrain**　Zhi Nan A boat with a sail is tethered in a pocket of shade from a bankside ancient tree; my walking stick walks me to the east of the bridge. My clothes are moist with drizzling of apricot blossoms, when I feel touching my face a tinge of cool from willowy wind. （张智中　译）

（122）登高（杜甫）

登高　杜甫	Climbing to the Height　Du Fu
风急天高猿啸哀，	Winds hurry sky high and apes moan sadly;
渚清沙白鸟飞回。	over pure islet with white sands birds wheel.
无边落木萧萧下，	Boundless forest sheds leaves shower by shower;
不尽长江滚滚来。	endless Yangtze rolls on from hour to hour.
万里悲秋常作客，	Before autumn scene, I am sentimental as a traveler;
百年多病独登台。	in my life pestered by illness, alone I climb the tower.
艰难苦恨繁霜鬓，	Through hardships and tribulations, I am white-crowned;
潦倒新停浊酒杯。	down and outcast, I give up my cup to drown sorrow.
	（张智中　译）

诗中，"无边落木萧萧下，不尽长江滚滚来"乃千古名句，许渊冲英译如下：

> The boundless forest sheds its leaves shower by shower;
>
> The endless river rolls its waves hour after hour.

多年前研读许渊冲先生，方知此译多年得来，并与卞之琳等有过切磋。译文音、形、义俱佳，确实难得的好译文。笔者的如上早期译文，明显受到其译文的影响。

晨读英文，读到这么一句：

> There shot up high into the air a fabulous fountain of trade deals and also funds, electronic dollars that fell earthwards like longed-for rain, like **a storm of spiralling autumn leaves**, like a vortex-blizzard of snowflakes **pouring down** into…(*The Cockroach* by Ian McEwan)

又读到一个英汉对照的句子：

> **The falling leaf spiralled** to the ground.
>
> 落叶盘旋著飘到了地上。

这里，a storm of spiralling autumn leaves 和 the falling leaf spiralled to the ground，形象生动，诗意充沛，恰与杜甫"无边落木萧萧下"可勾可连。借鉴之后，"无边落木萧萧下，不尽长江滚滚来"另译如下：

> A storm of spiralling autumn leaves are pouring down through the air;
>
> the speeding water of the Yangtze River is emptying itself into the sea.

整首诗改译如下：

Climbing to the Height　Du Fu

Winds hurry, sky high, apes

　　moan sadly; over an islet

　　　　pure with white sand, birds

are flying and wheeling. A

　　storm of spiraling autumn

　　　　leaves are pouring down

through the air; the speeding

　　water of the Yangtze River is

　　　　emptying itself into the sea.

Before boundless autumn

　　scene, I am sentimental as

　　　　a wanderer; in my life,

pestered by illness, alone

　　I climb the tower. Through

　　　　hardships and tribulations,

I am heavily silver-crowned;

　　down and outcast, I give up

　　　　the cup to drown my sorrow.

（张智中　译）

再读英文：

Towards evening **a violent storm of rain came on**, and **the wind was so high** that all the windows and doors in the old house shook and rattled. In fact, it was just such weather as he loved.

当天晚上，一场暴风雨大作。风刮得非常大，整幢老房子的窗户和门都在颤抖，还嘎吱作响。事实上，他就喜欢这样的天气。

And indeed for near a hundred miles together upon this coast we saw nothing but a waste, uninhabited country by day, and heard nothing but **howling and roaring of wild beasts** by night.

我们在沿岸行驶了大概一百英里。这其间，白天只见一片荒凉，不见人迹；晚上则只闻野兽的嚎叫和嘶吼。

He was sitting by the window, watching the ruined gold of **the yellowing trees fly through the air**, and **the red leaves dancing madly down** the long avenue.

他坐在窗户旁边，看着泛黄的树上落下的枯败的金叶在空中飞舞，红叶则沿着长长的林阴大道狂舞。

We come to a river **of swirling eddies**.

我们来到湍急的河边。

The bat flitted about them in silence; a bird roused from its nest by the light which glared up among the trees, **flew circling about the flame**.

蝙蝠无声地在他们身边飞来飞去，一只鸟儿由于树林中一闪一闪的亮光而从巢里惊飞起来，围着火焰盘旋。

For the next moment **a shower of** little pebbles **came rattling** in at the window

因为紧接着小鹅卵石像暴雨一样噼里啪啦地砸进窗户。

The course kept turning and turning in a narrow and **well-timbered valley**.

河道在狭窄而多木的山谷中千回百转。

The grass would be only **rustling in the wind**, and the pool **rippling to the waving of the reeds**.

草只会在风的吹动下沙沙作响，芦苇的摆动使得池水漾起了波纹。

Autumn passed thus. I saw, **with surprise and grief**, the leaves decay and fall, and **nature again assume the barren and bleak appearance it had worn** when I first beheld the woods and the lovely moon.

秋天就这样过去了。我惊奇而忧伤地望着树叶变黄、落下。大自然再次呈现出荒凉、凄冷的景象，就像去年我第一次看见树林和明月时的样子。

She moved out into the sunlight, and **through her red hair rippled the wind**.

她来到阳光底下，风轻轻吹拂着她的红发。

借鉴如上英文表达，杜甫《登高》另译如下，首先散体：

Height Climbing　　Du Fu

The wind and the sky are so high, when the sad howling and roaring of apes are heard; birds fly circling about the islet pure with white sand. In the boundlessly well-timbered forest, a violent storm of yellowing leaves comes on, a shower after another shower, flying through the air of swirling eddies, before dancing madly down, rustling and rippling to the waving of a mass of leaves. Through which the endless Long River keeps rushing and rolling. Autumn is thickening, when nature again assumes the barren and bleak appearance it has worn. As a lifelong solitary wanderer, I, afflicted with illnesses, see with sentimental grief the decaying and falling leaves while climbing to a greater height. Through hardships, through tribulations, and through my gray hair, the autumn wind is rippling, when I, down and out, stop the cup to drown my sorrow.

（张智中　译）

分行成为诗体：

Height Climbing　　Du Fu

The wind and the sky are so high,

　　when the sad howling and roaring

　　　　of apes are heard; birds fly circling

about the islet pure with white sand.

　　In the boundlessly well-timbered

　　　　forest, a violent storm of yellowing

leaves comes on, a shower after

　　another shower, flying through

　　　　the air of swirling eddies, before

dancing madly down, rustling and

　　rippling to the waving of a mass

of leaves. Through which the endless
Long River keeps rushing and rolling.
Autumn is thickening, when nature
again assumes the barren and bleak
appearance it has worn. As a lifelong
solitary wanderer, I, afflicted with
illnesses, see with sentimental grief
the decaying and falling leaves while
climbing to a greater height. Through
hardships, through tribulations, and
through my gray hair, the autumn wind
is rippling, when I, down and out,
stop the cup to drown my sorrow.

（张智中　译）

除了英文借鉴之外，译文中，through which the endless Long River keeps rushing and rolling，前后均为句号。这似乎不符合英文语法规则，但却是地道的英文，没有问题的。在多年的英文阅读中，笔者曾数次读到此类语言现象。例如：

Forty years had rolled by, long and rapid, dreary as a day of sadness and as similar as the hours of a sleepless night. Forty years of which nothing remained, not even a memory, not even a misfortune, since the death of his parents. Nothing.

四十年过去了，漫长而迅速，生活枯燥得就像一个个愁苦的白昼和失眠的漫漫长夜。四十年来，他什么也没留下，连一点回忆也没有，自从他的父母逝世以后，甚至一点不幸也没有。什么都没有。

在这个句子中，Forty years of which 中的 which，显然指上一个句子的内容，但前面却用了句号，而不是逗号。这种现象在语法书里没有解释，但笔者猜想，本来该用逗号，却使用了句号，该是因为句子太长，或者为了强调的缘故，才这样的吧。

（123）月下独酌（其一）（李白）

| 月下独酌（其一）
李白
花间一壶酒，
独酌无相亲。
举杯邀明月，
对影成三人。
月既不解饮，
影徒随我身。
暂伴月将影，
行乐须及春。
我歌月徘徊，
我舞影零乱。
醒时相交欢，
醉后各分散。
永结无情游，
相期邈云汉。 | **Three Midnight Drinkers: the Moon, Me, and My Shadow**
Li Bai
A pot of wine amid a riot
  of flowers, a lonely drinker,
    companionless. My cup
lifted moonward —
  dreamily, three drinkers
    now: the moon, me, and
my shadow. But the moon
  is no drinker and the shadow,
    a vain follower of me.
A shifty party of three,
  for a while, to while away
    night hours, merry-making
before springtime slips away.
  When I sing, the moon lingers
    and loiters; when I dance,
my shadow is tangled into
  a great mess. In sobriety, we
    carouse, revel, rave, and regale
ourselves; befuddled by drink,
  we scatter, like the wind scattering
    clouds from the sky. Our everlasting
friendship is privy to no mortals,
  and our next meeting will be sky-
    ward, beyond heaven of heavens.
（张智中　译） |

  原诗 14 行，译诗 24 行，多出整整 10 行。每 3 行一个单元，逐行缩进。诗行的调整，在古诗英译中，本为常见，尤其在西方人的古诗英译中，诗行变通更为常见。另外，译诗中有多处英文借鉴，例如：

Next year, we shall depict **a riot of flowers** on our calendar.

明年，我们的日历将会有五彩缤纷的花朵。

Dusk found her crying **companionless** in the streets.

黄昏的时候，她独自在街上哭泣。

She smiled, looking **dreamily** out on the shifty landscape.

她脸露微笑，用一种梦幻似的目光看着那变化莫测的景色。

But it's no problem for **shifty** workers to manage this.

不过游荡着的工人来管理这个一点都没问题。

这里，shifty 是形容词，大意："变化的；诡诈的；机智的。"

He **was tangled into** this situation by his debts.

他因为债务而卷入了这件事情。

The heavy rain made **a great mess** of the garden.

这场大雨把花园搞得一团糟。

Life looks better **in sobriety** and it will be better.

清醒的生活看来好多了，而且将会更好。

We **regaled ourselves** on caviar and champagne.

我们尽情地享用鱼子酱和香槟酒。

He was **befuddled by drink**.

他喝得迷迷糊糊的。

She **was** not **privy to** any information contained in the letters.

她未获准接触那些信的内容。

（124）春日（朱熹）

读英文：

He was alive to every new scene, joyful when he saw **the beauties of the setting sun**, and more happy when he beheld it rise and recommence a new day.

每个新景色都令他兴致盎然，夕阳之美令他欢喜；旭日东升更令他快乐，因为新的一天开始了。

Even broken in spirit as he is, no one can feel more deeply than he does **the beauties of nature**.

即便是像他一样情绪低落，也没有人能像他那样深深地领悟自然之美。

All Nature was wide awake and **stirring**, now.

此时自然界的万物全都醒来，充满了活力。

这里的形容词 stirring，为"活跃的；令人激动的"之意。

> The air was warm and balmy.
>
> 天气温暖宜人。

这里的形容词 balmy，为"芳香的；温和的"之意。

> It's almost like summertoday, balmy and warm.
>
> 今天天气暖融融的，就像夏天一样。

朱熹《春日》如下：

春日　朱熹

胜日寻芳泗水滨，

无边光景一时新。

等闲识得东风面，

万紫千红总是春。

借鉴如上英文表达，《春日》采取不同的诗行排列，有两种英译：

A Fine Day in Spring　Zhu Xi	**A Fine Day in Spring**　Zhu Xi
In a fine day I am 　in search of the beauties 　　of nature by River Sishui; the boundless view 　is stirring, heartening, 　　refreshing, uplifting. It is easy to descry 　the visage of spring: 　　a riot of colors are gorgeous in the east 　wind which is 　　warm and balmy. （张智中　译）	In a fine day I am in search of the beauties of nature by River Sishui; the boundless view is stirring, 　　　　heartening, 　　　　　　refreshing, 　　　　　　　　uplifting. It is easy to descry the visage of spring: a riot of colors are gorgeous in the east wind which is warm and balmy. （张智中　译）

（125）塞下曲（二）（卢纶）

读英文：

> **The arrow embedded itself deeply** in the door.
>
> 这支箭深深地嵌在了门上。

动词 embed 大意："（使）插入；（使）嵌入；深留脑中。"

An arrow whizzed past and stuck in a tree.

一支箭"飕"地一声飞过去，钉在一棵树上。

... on the other bank could be seen a black **mass** of trees, outlined against a stormy sky.

河的对岸，在风雨交加的天空的映衬下，人们只能够看到一片黑压压的树林。

The youthful maiden was entombed in the **massive** depths of the earth.

这个年轻的少女被隐藏在地底幽暗的深处。

卢纶《塞下曲（二）》英译：

塞下曲（二）　卢纶 林暗草惊风， 将军夜引弓。 平明寻白羽， 没在石棱中。	**Border Songs (No. 2)**　Lu Lun The grass in dark woods is startled by the wind, when the general draws his bow in the night, an arrow whizzing past to strike in something hard. The next morning he retraces 　　the plumed arrow, 　　　　which embeds itself 　　　　　　deeply in a 　　　　　　　　massive rock. （张智中　译）

（126）望洞庭（刘禹锡）

望洞庭　刘禹锡 湖光秋月两相和， 潭面无风镜未磨。 遥望洞庭山水翠， 白银盘里一青螺。	**The Sightly Dongting Lake**　Liu Yuxi The autumn moon and the shiny 　　lake delight each other; windless, 　　　the unruffled lake surface is like an unpolished bronze mirror. 　　The emerald mountain beyond 　　　Dongting Lake offers itself to view from afar: in green water 　it is suggestive of a green 　　spiral shell in a silver plate. （张智中　译）

译文中，offers itself to view 比较亮眼，这一表达借鉴于下面这个英文句子：

Soon the waves of the bay disappeared behind a bend of rising ground, and the Floridan "champagne" alone **offered itself to view**.

小湾的波浪很快就消失在了一片蜿蜒的高地后面，现在举目四望，都是佛罗里达的田野了。

其实，反身代词 itself 的使用，在英文中非常普遍。它不仅用于强调，还可给语言带来很好的美学效果。例如下面包含 itself 的英文句子：

The land breaks **itself** into little knolls, and the sea runs up, hither and thither, in a thousand creeks and inlets.

岛上的陆地由许多小丘组成，经过海水冲刷，形成了无数的小溪和水湾。

The chance which now seems lost may present **itself** at the last moment.

现在看上去丧失的机会，可能会在最后的时刻出现。

The thought forced **itself** upon him.

这个思想又挤进了他的脑袋。

Then this little seed will stretch **itself** and begin—timidly at first—to push a charming little sprig inoffensively upward toward the sun.

之后，这颗小小的种子使劲地向上钻，开始还有些胆怯，后来则奋力长出一片可爱的小嫩芽，乖乖地向着太阳看齐。

Her rectitude of thinking delighted my judgment; the sweetness of her nature wrapped **itself** around my heart; and then her young and tender and budding loveliness, sent a delicious madness to my brain.

她思想正直，说明我没看错人；她的柔情萦绕在我的心间；她那年轻、亲切而含苞待放的娇美使我痴狂。

And this, terrible enough in **itself**, was accompanied by suffering.

这种感觉本身已经很可怕了，却还要伴随着疼痛的折磨。

The village emptied **itself**, and a motley crowd trooped out to meet him, men in the forefront, with bows and spears clutched menacingly, and women and children faltering timidly in the rear.

整个村子的人都出来了，各色人等都成群结队地出来见他。男人在前面威胁地紧抓着弓和矛，妇女和孩子在后边怯生生地挪动着步子。

Then everything will certainly explain **itself**.

那时，所有的事情都肯定会真相大白。

The ticking of the clock began to bring **itself** into notice.

渐渐可以注意到时钟的滴答声。

This, in **itself**, did not amount to much.

这件事本身没什么大不了。

A section of the mob tore **itself** loose and surged in after her.

有一部分暴民离开了队伍，跟着她涌了进来。

The fact spoke for **itself**; it was a strange, horrible, uncanny thing.

事实不言而喻，这是件奇怪、令人震惊、不可思议的事情。

Said the cardinal in a tone of vexation, through which, however, a sort of esteem manifested **itself**.

红衣主教的语气有些气恼，可是还流露出一丝敬意。

His eyes narrowed to laughing slits of blue, his face wreathed **itself** in joy, and his mouth curled in a smile as he cried aloud.

他的眼睛笑眯眯地成了一条蓝线，满脸笑容，嘴角也笑着翘起来，同时大声喊。

By noon the storm had spent **itself**, and by six in the evening the waves had died down sufficiently to let Chris leave the helm.

到中午时，风暴已经势穷而停了下来；到傍晚六点，海浪已经基本平息，克里斯可以离开舵轮了。

（127）竹石（郑燮）

竹石　郑燮	**A Bamboo Biting in the Rock**　Zheng Xie
咬定青山不放松，	of the green mountain is
立根原在破岩中。	deeply rooted in the crevice.
千磨万击还坚劲，	Windswept,
任尔东西南北风。	weathered,
	weather-beaten,

weather-worn,

it is still strong

and sturdy,

in spite of winds

from the north

or the south

or the east

or the west.

（张智中　译）

译诗中，标题与正文之间，形成跨行。译诗散读：A bamboo biting in the rock of the green mountain is deeply rooted in the crevice. Windswept, weathered, weather-beaten, weather-worn, it is still strong and sturdy, in spite of winds from the north or the south or the east or the west.

由两个句子构成，一气呵成。头韵明显，三个 or 之外，windswept, weathered, weather-beaten, weather-worn, 连用四个充分头韵的复合词，带来一泄而下之坚定语气。

（128）春雪（韩愈）

读英文：

There is a great thaw and a bending, a sound of running waters, and **a budding and sprouting of green things**. And there is drumming of partridges, and songs of robins, and great music, for the winter is broken.

大片的雪融化了，拐弯处，流水叮咚响，绿色植物在抽枝发芽。那里有山鹑鼓翅的声音，知更鸟的歌声，有美妙的音乐，因为冬天已经结束。

It was an abyss of **green beauty** and shady depths, pierced by vagrant shafts of the sun and mottled here and there by the sun's broader blazes.

这是一个深渊，里面绿叶茂密，阴凉处深不可测，但却被太阳游移不定的光线划破了，如火焰一般的太阳光把四处照得斑驳陆离。

There is a sort of prettiness about these islands which, though it never rises to **the loveliness of romantic scenery**, is nevertheless

attractive in its way.

这片群岛的风景之美，虽算不上富有浪漫色彩，但却有着自己独到的迷人之处。

春雪　韩愈 新年都未有芳华， 二月初惊见草芽。 白雪却嫌春色晚， 故穿庭树作飞花。	**Spring Snow**　Han Yu The advent of the New Year fails to exhibit any beauty of green things; the third moon is startled to see young grass stem 　　　　　　pushing, 　　　　　　　　budding, 　　　　　　　　　　sprouting…. Snowflakes hate the late coming of spring: they fall and 　　　　　　fly, as blossoms, 　　　　　　　　　through courtyard trees — the loveliness of romantic scenery is attractive in its way. （张智中　译）

（129）离思五首（四）（元稹）

读英文：

The **seafarer** looked at him with the suspicion of a wink.
航海家看着他，朝他眨了眨眼睛表示怀疑。

The **sightseer** watches you from the balcony.
看风景人在楼上看你。

Over the lake was a blue sky with **fluffy clouds**.
湖泊的上空是点缀着朵朵白云的蓝天。

形容词 fluffy，意为"绒毛般的，覆有绒毛的；（食物等）松软的，透气的"等。

It bears **clusters** of mauve flowers in early summer.
初夏时节，它开出了一簇簇淡紫色的花儿。

She **darted a look at** him when he was coming in.
他走进来时，她瞟了他一眼。

离思五首（四）　元稹 曾经沧海难为水， 除却巫山不是云。 取次花丛懒回顾， 半缘修道半缘君。	**Five Poems on My Strong Feeling of Affection (No. 4)** Yuan Zhen No water is water — 　for a seafarer 　　who has seen the sea 　　　overflowing with water; no clouds are clouds 　for a sightseer who 　　has seen Wushan Mountain 　　　veiled in fluffy clouds. Strolling through flowery 　clusters, I do not deign 　　to dart a single loving look — partly out of my religious cultivation, 　partly out of my strong 　　feeling of affection for you. （张智中　译）

（130）村居（高鼎）

读英文：

There is a great thaw and a bending, a sound of running waters, and **a budding and sprouting of green things**. And there is drumming of partridges, and songs of robins, and great music, for the winter is broken.

大片的雪融化了，拐弯处，流水叮咚响，绿色植物在抽枝发芽。那里有山鹑鼓翅的声音，知更鸟的歌声，有美妙的音乐，因为冬天已经结束。

这个句子在韩愈《春雪》的英译中，已经用过，但这里仍可借鉴。

He **was discharged from** the army following his injury.
他受伤后就退伍了。

She **was discharged from** the police force for bad conduct.
她因行为不轨被清除出警察队伍。

In less than a year after the commencement of the works, **toward**

the close of September, the gigantic reflector rose into the air to a height of 280 feet.

九月底，工程开始仅仅不到一年时间，这架高 280 英尺、直入云霄的庞大反射镜就建成了。

村居　高鼎	**Village Life in Early Spring**　Gao Ding
草长莺飞二月天， 拂堤杨柳醉春烟。 儿童散学归来早， 忙趁东风放纸鸢。	The third moon sees budding 　　and sprouting of green things, 　　　over which orioles and warblers are flitting and flying. 　　Drooping willows are waving 　　　and swaying in the intoxicating mist suffusing the river bank. 　　Schoolchildren, discharged 　　　from their classroom, lose no time flying kites in the spring 　　wind, before the close of 　　　a day so fair and fine. 　　（张智中　译）

"二月"，英译为 the third moon（三月），因为古人只用阴历，译为英文，则为阳历。因此，后推一个月才对。多数古诗英译，见到月份，都是照直翻译，错误而不自知矣。

（131）城东早春（杨巨源）

读英文：

One day in early spring he had so far relaxed as to go for a walk with me in the Park, where **the first faint shoots of green were breaking out upon the elms**, and the sticky spear-heads of the chestnuts **were just beginning to burst into** their five fold leaves.

早春的一天，福尔摩斯清闲起来，居然有时间陪我去公园散步，公园里的榆树已经抽出嫩绿的幼芽，栗树梢头也开始冒出五瓣形新叶。

城东早春　杨巨源 诗家清景在新春， 绿柳才黄半未匀。 若待上林花似锦， 出门俱是看花人。	**Early Spring View East of the City**　Yang Juyuan Fresh early spring is the poets' 　　favorite: the first faint shoots of green are just beginning 　　to break out upon the willows, into their yellow and green, 　　a color still uneven. When the capital is noisy and full-blown 　　with blossoms, streets and avenues, big and small, are 　　thronged with flower admirers. 　　　　　　　（张智中　译）

（132）访人不遇留别馆（李商隐）

读英文：

He always wants to be my **pal**, you know.
他一直想成为我的朋友，你知道。

Flowers seem to speak a welcoming message to the **splendid spring**.
花儿似乎在对这美妙的春天表达着欢迎的讯息。

We spent the afternoon **traipsing** from one shop to another.
我们用了一下午的时间逛了一家又一家商店。

Our young noblemen are bred from their childhood **in idleness** and luxury; that, as soon as years will permit, they consume their vigour, and contract odious diseases among lewd females.
我们的年轻贵族从孩子时代起就过着游手好闲、奢侈豪华的生活；成年以后，他们就在淫荡的女人中消耗精力，并染上一身恶病。

This beautiful room **is bathed in** light. You'll wake up every morning in a good humor.
这个漂亮的房间沐浴着阳光，每天早上醒来时你就会有个好心情。

| 访人不遇留别馆
李商隐
卿卿不惜锁窗春，
去作长楸走马身。
闲倚绣帘吹柳絮，
日高深院断无人。 | **Staying at an Inn After Failure to Be Taken in by a Friend**
Li Shangyin
Oh my loving friend, oh
  my beloved pal, why, instead
    of cherishing a gardenful of
splendid spring, should you,
  riding a horse, trudge and traipse
    along a long way lined with
      lingering catalpa trees?

In helpless idleness, I lean
  against the balustrade fanned
    by the wind-blown embroidered
curtain of the inn, where fluffy
  catkin pieces are dancing
    in the languid air, to fix my gaze
on the yonder deep yard, which,
  deserted by you, is bathed in
    lonely sunlight and vacant spring.
（张智中　译） |

（133）雪梅（卢梅坡）

读英文：

The snow showed **no sign of** melting.

雪没有一点融化的迹象。

Headaches may be **a sign of** stress.

头痛可能是紧张的迹象。

Humidity is **a measure of** moisture in the atmosphere.

湿度是空气内含水分多少的量度。

That is **a measure of** how bad things have become at the bank.

那就是银行的局面已经糟糕到何种程度的衡量标准。

| 雪梅　卢梅坡
梅雪争春未肯降，
骚人搁笔费评章。
梅须逊雪三分白， | **Mume Flowers & Snowy Blossoms**　Lu Meipo
The first sign of early spring:
  mume flowers,
    or snowy blossoms? |

雪却输梅一段香。	Still an open question, 　　when the poet is 　　　　a clumsy judge. Mume flowers are inferior 　　to snowy blossoms in 　　　　a stretch of white; snowy blossoms are inferior 　　to mume flowers in 　　　　a measure of fragrance. 　　　　（张智中　译）

比较许渊冲的英译：

Mume and Snow (I)　Lu Meipo

The mume blossoms and snow vie in announcing spring;

A poet knows not in whose praises he should sing.

The mume blossoms are not so white as winter snow;

In fragrance snow can't match mume blossoms when they blow.

（许渊冲　译）[97]

（134）梅花（崔道融）

梅花　崔道融 数萼初含雪， 孤标画本难。 香中别有韵， 清极不知寒。 横笛和愁听， 斜枝倚病看。 朔风如解意， 容易莫摧残。	**Mume Blossoms**　Cui Daorong The budding green 　　of mume blossoms 　　　　is caught in snow; its rare beauty defies 　　painting by any 　　　　dexterous hand. Overflowing with 　　refined scent 　　　　and elegant charm, the blossoms, 　　purity itself, are 　　　　insensible of the cold. The rising and falling

97 许渊冲，许渊冲译千家诗：汉文、英文［Z］，北京：中译出版社，2021：173。

	fluting is travelling
	        in lingering sorrow;
	the branches are
	    an eyeful when
	        gnarly and gnarled.
	North wind, please
	    be obliging and
	        accommodating
	— be a blower and
	    preserver, instead
	        of a destroyer.
	（张智中　译）

译文借鉴了两处英文：

I am not **insensible of** your concern.

我不是没察觉到你的忧虑。

形容词 insensible 的意思，是"无感觉的；麻木的；无动于衷的"。

She's quite **an eyeful**!

她真是个美人！

另外，译文最后的 blower，preserver 和 destroyer，不仅发挥英文-er 后缀类词汇的优势，还令人想起雪莱《西风颂》中的两行：

Wild Spirit, which art moving everywhere;

Destroyer and preserver; hear, oh, hear!

英文诗行的亮点，也在 destroyer 和 preserver 这两个单词的运用。多数译者汉译为"摧毁者"和"破坏者"，太过拘泥。汉诗英译之时，比如崔道融之《梅花》，诗中似乎没有什么"摧毁者"和"破坏者"的影子，却使用 destroyer 和 preserver，再加上 blower，三词并用，更添其趣。此乃深层之译。

（135）满江红（岳飞）

读英文：

At this remark, Ardan **pushed up his shock of red hair**; he saw that he was on the point of being involved in a struggle with this person upon the very gist of the whole question. He looked sternly at him in his turn and said.

听到这里，阿当红色的头发都竖起来了，他意识到要和这个人在最关键的问题上争个你死我活了。他也虎视眈眈地望着对方，回敬道。

She waited nervously for his anger to **subside**.

她提心吊胆地等他的怒气平息下来。

The storm began to **subside**.

风暴渐渐平息了。

His brows were drawn into two hard black lines, while **his eyes shone** out from beneath them **with a steely glitter**.

他眉头紧锁，形成了两道粗粗的黑线，眉毛下面那双眼睛射出刚毅的光芒。

满江红　岳飞	The River Red Through　Yue Fei
怒发冲冠，凭阑处，潇潇雨歇。 抬望眼，仰天长啸，壮怀激烈。 三十功名尘与土，八千里路云和月。 莫等闲，白了少年头，空悲切。 靖康耻，犹未雪； 臣子恨，何时灭。 驾长车，踏破贺兰山缺。 壮志饥餐胡虏肉，笑谈渴饮匈奴血。 待从头，收拾旧山河，朝天阙。	Rage pushes up my shock of hair; my brows are drawn into two hard black lines. Leaning against the balustrade, I see the heavy rain subside. Looking skyward, my eyes shining out from beneath them with a steely glitter, I cannot help heaving a long sigh: I am still excited and ambitious for achievement. Thirty years of struggling, all in vain: like dirt; through eight thousand miles of journey, a wandering life of clouds and moon. Don't linger and loiter: a boyish crown grays soon; wait not to be regretful and sorrowful. The shame of national subjugation has not been avenged; how can a subject's hate be thoroughly quenched?

	Driving a chariot, I'll charge for Helan Mountain to have it levelled. Filled with ambition, I'll eat the flesh of my enemy when hungry; talking and laughing, I'll drink the blood of my foe when thirsty. Wait till I have recovered our lost land, I'll report the victorious news to my lord! （张智中　译）

比较许渊冲的英译：

Tune: The River All Red　Yue Fei

Wrath sets on end my hair,

I lean on railings where

I see the drizzling rain has ceased.

Raising my eyes

Towards the skies,

I heave long sighs,

My wrath not yet appeased.

To dust is gone the fame achieved in thirty years;

Like cloud-veiled moon the thousand-mile land disappears.

Should youthful heads in vain turn grey,

We would regret for aye.

Lost our capitals,

What a burning shame!

How can we generals

Quench our vengeful flame!

Driving our chariots of war, we'd go

To break through our relentless foe.

Valiantly we'd cut off each head;

Laughing, we'd drink the blood they shed.

When we've reconquered our lost land,

In triumph would return our army grand.

（许渊冲　译）⁹⁸

（136）江畔独步寻花（六）（杜甫）

读英文：

Eaglet bent down its head to hide a smile; some of **the other birds tittered** audibly.

然后小鹰低下头窃笑；其他的一些鸟也禁不住偷笑出声来。

动词 titter，有"窃笑；傻笑；嗤笑"之意，想起杜甫"自在娇莺恰恰啼"，或许可用。

江畔独步寻花（六） 杜甫 黄四娘家花满蹊， 千朵万朵压枝低。 留连戏蝶时时舞， 自在娇莺恰恰啼。	**Strolling along the River in Search of Flowers (No. 6)** Du Fu The path leading to 　　the home of Huang Siniang 　　　　is choked with flowers, which are low with 　　myriads of flowering 　　　　twigs upon twigs. Frolicking butterflies 　　are dancing from 　　　　time to time; self-satisfied yellow 　　orioles are tittering and 　　　　twittering now and then. （张智中　译）

（137）饮湖上初晴后雨（苏轼）

读英文：

The waves **were dimpling in the sunshine**.

波浪在阳光下泛起笑涡。

---

98 许渊冲，汉英对照宋词三百首［Z］，北京：高等教育出版社，2004：471-473。

All the air flashed and sparkled, and the snow was diamond dust.

周围的空气闪烁炫目，雪就像钻石磨成的粉末。

饮湖上初晴后雨　苏轼	The West Lake: Sunny or Rainy　Su Shi
水光潋滟晴方好， 山色空濛雨亦奇。 欲把西湖比西子， 淡妆浓抹总相宜。	Sunny, the waves are dimpling 　in the sunshine, all the air flashes 　　and sparkles; rainy, surrounding hills are hazy and misty — 　a constantly wonderful scene. 　　The West Lake can be compared to an ancient beauty, whose beauty 　is in the eye of the beholder: 　　made-up light or heavy. （张智中　译）

（138）鹧鸪天·桂花（李清照）

读英文：

Her **disposition was affectionate**.

她性情柔和。

This is a village **remote from the madding crowd**.

这是一个远离喧嚣尘世的村庄。

He is not one to **parade** his achievements.

他不是一个爱炫耀自己成就的人。

His new house **was the envy of** all his friends.

他的新居成了所有朋友羡慕的对象。

She was **extolled** as a genius.

她被誉为天才。

鹧鸪天·桂花　李清照	**Tune: Partridge in the Sky**
暗淡轻黄体性柔， 情疏迹远只香留。 何须浅碧深红色， 自是花中第一流。 梅定妒，菊应羞， 画阑开处冠中秋。	**Osmanthus Flowers**　Li Qingzhao Of varying shades of yellow: dark, light, and tender, Osmanthus flowers are with an affectionately bashful disposition. Cassia trees, far from the madding crowd,

骚人可煞无情思， 何事当年不见收？	grow unrestrained while emanating lingering fragrance; no need for you to parade autumn in your light green and deep red, retiring, you are the flower of flowers. As the envy of mume flowers, you put to shame chrysanthemum flowers; in the garden enclosed with colorfully carved railings, as a magic bloomer through mid-autumn, you are matchless and peerless. Qu Yuan, father of Chinese poetry, heartful or heartless? —— in your Departing Sorrow, why Osmanthus flowers are not extolled? （张智中　译）

（139）夏意（苏舜钦）

读英文：

After a few days, the **flowers**, like a **raging** fire, are burning in all directions.

过了几天，花儿像熊熊烈火似的向四面八方燃烧着。

They all sit on the dirt in the **dappled** shade of a tree.

他们都坐在斑驳的树荫下的地上。

Her speech **was punctuated by** bursts of applause.

她的讲演不时被阵阵掌声打断。

The silence of the night **was punctuated by** the distant rumble of traffic.

夜晚的宁静被远处车辆的隆隆声所打破。

They saw the **intermittent** flashes from a lighthouse.

他们看见了灯塔发出一闪一灭的光。

He has **intermittent** bursts of interest.

他的兴趣是一阵阵的。

夏意　苏舜钦	**Summer**　Su Shunqin
别院深深夏席清， 石榴开遍透帘明。 树阴满地日当午， 梦觉流莺时一声。	The deep yard is dotted with a bamboo mat which is clear and cool; the curtain is crystal bright with raging pomegranate blossoms. The high noon sees the ground dappled in light and shade, when the dream is punctuated by the intermittent twitters of orioles. 　　　（张智中　译）

（140）题葡萄图（徐渭）

读英文：

Draggy sales are attributed to a psychology of caution.

拖泥带水的销售归咎于谨慎的心理。

But I was surprised, when coming to **my heap of grapes**, which were **so rich and fine** when I **gathered** them, **to find them all spread about, trod to pieces, and dragged about, some here, some there**, and abundance eaten and devoured.

　　但是，令我惊讶的是，当我回到葡萄堆时，却发现我之前堆在一起的又多又好的葡萄散落一地，被踩得支离破碎，还被拖得到处都是，这里一点那里一点的，还有很多被吃掉了。

题葡萄图　徐渭	**Inscription on a Painting of Grapes**　Xu Wei
半生落魄已成翁， 独立书斋啸晚风。 笔底明珠无处卖， 闲抛闲掷野藤中。	Down and out for half a life- 　　time, I am an old man now. 　　Alone in my lone study, I face the evening breeze. 　　A draggy sale: heaps of

> black-pearl-like grapes,
> so rich and fine, are found
>   all spread about, trod to
>   pieces, some here, some
> there, as harvest from beneath
>   my brush, in and into,
>   grapevine of wild vegetation.
> （张智中　译）

（141）丑奴儿·书博山道中壁（辛弃疾）

读英文：

And then, for the slender **lad** of fifteen or sixteen that he appeared, there was a vague, insinuating fullness about the figure, which did not fail to corroborate my suspicions.

而且，尽管他看上去是一个十五六岁的瘦弱少年，他的身材却隐隐地有些丰满，这一切更加证实了我的怀疑。

During my youthful days **discontent never visited my mind**, and if **I was ever overcome by ennui, the sight of what is beautiful in nature** or the study of what is excellent and sublime in the productions of man **could always interest my heart and communicate elasticity to my spirits**.

青春年少时，我从未觉得不满足。即便有时我感觉无聊，但只要看见大自然的美丽景色，或是体味一下文学作品之美，我总能变得兴致勃勃，心情开朗。

On the spot, accordingly, in the pleasant hall and with her eyes on me, I, **for a reason that I couldn't then have phrased**, achieved an inward resolution — offered a vague pretext for my lateness and, with the plea of the beauty of the night and of the heavy dew and wet feet, went as soon as possible to my room.

在舒适的大厅里，她一直看着我，我当时也说不清为什么，决定找个含糊的理由来解释晚归，说美丽夜色惹人喜爱，露水太大，打湿了鞋子，便匆匆忙忙回自己房间了。

| 丑奴儿·书博山道中壁
辛弃疾

少年不识愁滋味，
爱上层楼。
爱上层楼，
为赋新词强说愁。
而今识尽愁滋味，
欲说还休。
欲说还休，
却道天凉好个秋！ | **Written on the Wall on My Way to Boshan**
To the Tune of "Song of Ugly Slave"　By Xin Qiji

As a lad sorrow never
　　visits my mind — it is a
stranger to me. I love
　　ascending the stairs,
more stairs, to a great
　　and greater height,
to feign sorrow to produce
　　lovey-dovey literary pieces.
Nowadays I am often
　　overcome by ennui and
grief, and the sight of what
　　is beautiful in nature
from a great height fails
　　to interest my heart and
communicate elasticity
　　to my spirits — for a reason
that I cannot phrase,
　　but I only sigh with feeling:
oh, what — what an autumn
　　— it's crisp and cool!
（张智中　译） |

（142）马诗二十三首（四）（李贺）

读英文：

He was **a good, solid horse, solid on his legs**.

这是一匹强壮的好马，四肢稳健。

They talked, **sitting their gaunt horses** in the dark.

他们坐在自己瘦骨嶙峋的马上，在黑暗里交谈。

He had the only **steady horse** of the lot.

他骑着这批马里唯一一匹结实的。

The word has **a brazen metallic quality** as if their throats were

phonograph horns.

这个词带有一种刺耳的金属音质，就像他们的喉咙是留声机喇叭一样。

形容词 brazen，意为"厚颜无耻的；明目张胆的；响而刺耳的；黄铜的"。

李贺《马诗二十三首（四）》英译，并比较许渊冲的英译：

| 马诗二十三首（四）
李贺
此马非凡马，
房星本是星。
向前敲瘦骨，
犹自带铜声。 | **Twenty-Three Poems on Horses (No. 4)**   Li He

The horse, good
  and solid on its
    legs, is an immortal
one, as a star
  symbolic of a
    heavenly horse.
When its bony frame
  is knocked, the steady
    voice of a brazen
metallic quality is
  produced, in spite
    of its gauntness.
（张智中　译） | **Horse Poems (Four Selections)**
Li He

IV
This is no ordinary steed
But an incarnate star indeed.
When I tap his bony frame, what's found?
I seem to hear metallic sound.
（许渊冲　译）[99] |

（143）金乡送韦八之西京（李白）

读英文：

The **route** was once much **travelled** but has fallen into disuse.

这条路线旅行的人以前常走，但是现在已不用了。

He will **escort** you through the forest.

他护送你穿过森林。

Nell looked up hastily, seized the young man's hand, and gazed so fixedly into his eyes that **his feelings were stirred to their depths**.

内尔急忙抬起头，紧紧地抓着他的手，目不转睛地盯着他，这激发了哈里内心深处的情感。

---

99 许渊冲，唐诗三百首：汉英对照［Z］，北京：海豚出版社，2013：173。

金乡送韦八之西京　李白	**Bidding Farewell to My Friend**　Li Bai
客自长安来， 还归长安去。 狂风吹我心， 西挂咸阳树。 此情不可道， 此别何时遇。 望望不见君， 连山起烟雾。	You are from the capital city 　　and now back to the capital city you go; my heart is blown by 　　the wild wind, which bears my heart away, westward, along 　　the route to be travelled by you, among the trees which line the 　　road to escort you. My feelings, stirred to their depths, are 　　unutterable, unspeakable, untellable — now I bid farewell to you, 　　wishing you fare well, but when — when can we meet again? 　　Your west-going form is retreating, gradually fading out of my sight, 　　when misty hills rise upon foggy hills. （张智中　译）

（144）十六字令三首（毛泽东）

读英文：

Don't **cling to** the kerb when you're driving.
不要紧贴路边开车。

A great swell, surge, or undulating mass, as of smoke or sound.
似巨浪翻腾巨浪、波涛或波浪形团块，如烟雾或声音。

He was killed **in the heat of** the action.
他在战斗最激烈时阵亡了。

He picked his way from muskeg to muskeg, and followed the other man's footsteps along and across the rocky ledges which **thrust** like islets through the sea of moss.
他小心翼翼地穿过一片又一片的沼泽地，顺着比尔的脚印往前走，跨过大片苔藓里如小岛般突起的岩石。

十六字令三首　毛泽东	**Three Poems of Sixteen Chinese Characters**　Mao Zedong
其一	I
山，	Peaks!
快马加鞭未下鞍。	upon which steeds gallop, mounted with riders;
惊回首，	a backward glance,
离天三尺三。	to find them cling to the sky.
其二	II
山，	Peaks,
倒海翻江卷巨澜。	a great swell, surge, and undulating mass of seawater;
奔腾急，	seething, foaming, and frothing,
万马战犹酣。	myriads of steeds in the heat of fighting.
其三	III
山，	Peaks
刺破青天锷未残。	thrust heavenward like unblunted swords;
天欲堕，	the sky would collapse,
赖以拄其间。	but for their support.
	（张智中　译）

（145）道旁木（唐备）

读英文：

Tom looked in the direction that the stranger pointed, and beheld **one of the great trees, fair and flourishing without, but rotten at the core**, and saw that it had been nearly hewn through, so that the first high wind was likely to blow it down.

汤姆朝陌生人指的方向望去，看到一棵大树，虽然美丽茂盛，树心却腐烂了，看得出它已经几乎被砍断了，所以一阵大风就能把它吹倒。

这句话令人想起唐备的《道旁木》来。原译及改译如下：

道旁木　唐备	**A Roadside Tree**　Tang Bei	**A Roadside Tree**　Tang Bei
狂风拔倒树，	The tree is uprooted	is uprooted by a gale,
树倒根已露。	by a gale: the root	its root revealed:
上有数枝藤，	is left open in the air.	fair and flourishing
青青犹未悟。	A few creepers on it	without with a few
	are still green:	creepers which are

	they are unaware of their status. （张智中　译）	still lushly green, it is already rotten at the core. （张智中　译）

改译后，采用了诗歌的跨题技法。散读如下：

A roadside tree is uprooted by a gale, its root revealed: fair and flourishing without with a few creepers which are still lushly green, it is already rotten at the core.

头韵明显，而且，副词 without 表示树的外表，介词 with 表示伴随，两个单词连用，形成颇耐回味的音义双关效果。整体而言，改译显有进步。

（146）秋兴八首（其一）（杜甫）

秋兴八首（其一）　　杜甫 玉露凋伤枫树林， 巫山巫峡气萧森。 江间波浪兼天涌， 塞上风云接地阴。 从菊两开他日泪， 孤舟一系故园心。 寒衣处处催刀尺， 白帝城高急暮砧。	白露似刀 　　凋残了枫树林， 巫山巫峡 　　峰峦蔽日寒气萧森。 大江 　　波浪汹涌触天空， 塞上 　　风云狂飙卷地动。 只身久滞一地两次看到菊花开 　　不禁难以抑止伤心的泪雨淋， 如孤舟系在江中啊 　　我的心总拴挂在故园的西亭。 处处秋寒 　　像刀尺刮动薄衣刺人身， 白帝城高 　　暮色沉黑如冰冷的铁砧。[100]
Ode to Autumn　Du Fu The pearllike dewdrops wither maples in red dye; The Gorge and Cliffs of Witch exhale dense fog around. Waves of upsurging river seem to storm the	**Autumn Inspiration (one of eight poems)**　Du Fu Maple trees, bitten by dew 　　of deep autumn, are wilting 　　　　and withering; Witching Mountain and Witching

100 袁运，唐宋名诗新译 [C]，海口：南海出版公司，1992：326-327。

sky; Dark clouds o'er mountains touch their shadows on the ground. Twice full-blown, asters blown off draw tears from the eye; Once tied up, lonely boat ties up my heart home-bound, Thinking of winter robes being made far and nigh, I hear at dusk but nearby washing blocks fast pound. （许渊冲 译）101	Gorge are enveloped in 　　mist eerie and uncanny. In the great river billows 　　sweep through the air, 　　　　dashing against the sky, where the clouds, murky 　　and gloomy, seem to scrape 　　　　the boundless earth. Twice chrysanthemum flowers 　　bloom and twice I shed 　　　　copious tears as a wanderer in a strange place; the lonely 　　tethered boat fails to tether 　　　　my homesick heart. At eventide the White Emperor 　　Town is noisy with clothes 　　　　beating on the anvil; from door to door women are busy 　　making warm clothes against 　　　　the approaching winter. （张智中 译）

　　袁运的今译，采取了自由诗的形式，为我们理解原诗提供了参考。许渊冲采取格律体译诗，用语一般；笔者采取自由体译诗，汲取英文优势，而致译文语言之醇厚耐味。

　　王树槐曾就此诗的译文阅读效果，找了五位英美专家进行阅读效果调查，译文包括三种：美国翻译家 Black，英国汉学家 Graham，以及笔者的译文，结果笔者的译文受到高度评价。大致说来，笔者的英文借鉴如下：

　　英译中，wilting，withering，witching，三个单词，头韵简尾韵，发挥了英文的优势，英美专家对此予以肯定。

　　单词 uncanny，可参见下面两个英文句子：

　　The silence was **uncanny**.

　　静得出奇。

　　I had an **uncanny** feeling of being watched.

101 许渊冲，唐诗三百首：汉英对照［Z］，北京：海豚出版社，2013：99。

我有一种奇怪的感觉，好像有人监视我。

接下来，译文 billows sweep through the air，介词 through 非常形象，发挥了英文介词形象生动的优势。例如下面的英文句子：

Billows of flame **swept through** the forest.

熊熊烈火席卷森林。

另外，译文 dashing against the sky 中的动词 dash，看似简单，其实形象贴切。例如：

The billow of the Atlantic **dash** high on the rock during a storm.

暴风雨时，大西洋的巨浪冲撞岩石掀得很高很高。

再看《秋兴八首（其一）》Black 的英译及笔者的回译。

AUTUMN Jade dew of autumn pearls the grove of withered maples; Silence and desolation brood over mountain and gorge. Wave after wave of the swiftly-flowing river rises to meet the sky as over the lofty passes clouds race before the wind to catch their shadows on the earth below. Chrysanthemums grow rank, like twice-shed tears – a second time in bloom. Here though my lonely boat is tied my heart looks back to its old home. Everywhere, with scissors and measure they hurry the winter robes as sunset touches the soaring walls of Po-ti to the hurried pounding of the washing-stones. （Black 译）	秋天玉润的露水， 珠子般网结于凋零的小树林中。 寂静与萧瑟面对， 巫山巫峡在沉沉沉思。 河流湍急，一浪接一浪， 升空接天； 高耸的巫山之巅， 云逃逸在风之前—— 试图抓住其投射在大地之影。 菊花怒放，一如 泪水两次落下——再次泪水成花。 这里，虽然孤舟独系， 我的心呀，念想着故园老家。 此处，彼处，剪裁度量： 人们在赶制着冬衣—— 当落日触及白帝之城， 那飞翔的高墙， 伴着洗衣石上传来急促的捣衣之声。 （张智中　译）

"玉露凋伤枫树林"，Black 的英译，Jade dew of autumn / pearls the grove of withered maples。译文似乎不太好理解。其实，此处的 pearl，当做动词，否则语言不通。

查词典：Pearl: vt. 珠子般散布于。vi. 成珠状。例如：

Tiny beads of perspiration are **pearling** his brow.

他的额上渗出了细粒汗珠。

Rain **pearled** down the window.

雨珠顺着窗户淌下。

回顾译文，方知译者措词之妙。回译汉语：

秋天玉润的露水，

珠子般网结于凋零的小树林中。

诗意丰盈矣。

"巫山巫峡气萧森"英译：

Silence and desolation brood / over mountain and gorge.（寂静与
萧瑟面对，巫山巫峡在沉沉沉思。）

视觉变化，想不到的译文。

译文中，动词 brood，搭配介词 over，表达效果颇佳。brood: v. 孵；沉思；
笼罩。brood over: 郁闷地沉思；沮丧地苦想。例如：

It's no use **brooding over** one's past mistakes.

老是抱着过去的错误是没用的。

Don't **brood over** lost opportunities.

别为失去的机会懊丧不已。

She **brooded over** her failure.

她为失败而郁郁沉思。

回顾译文：

Silence and desolation brood

over mountain and gorge.

无灵主语（Silence and desolation）与有灵动词（brood over）搭配，两行
之间形成跨行。译文乃是地道之英文诗行。

"江间波浪兼天涌，塞上风云接地阴。"英译：

Wave after wave of the swiftly-flowing river

rises to meet the sky

as over the lofty passes

clouds race before the wind

to catch their shadows on the earth below.

显然，原诗二行，译诗却是五行，打破了开始的一行译两行的规律。译者所忠实的，不是原诗的诗行，而是杜甫之诗情，以及英诗之建行：自然而然，不加雕琢。

Wave after wave，写波涛不绝，发挥英文之优势；swiftly-flowing river，看似平凡，却不是一般译者所能造出；rises to meet the sky（波浪连绵直向天），平淡措语，却力度非凡。随后，着一 as，将上下两句合并，打通一气，淋漓而酣畅。

"寒衣处处催刀尺，白帝城高急暮砧。"英译：

Everywhere, with scissors and measure

they hurry the winter robes

as sunset touches

the soaring walls of Po-ti

to the hurried pounding of the washing-stones.

译文极富动态之美。touches，出人意料之外；soaring，城墙也飞动，诗意顿生；hurried pounding，用语洗练而形象；washing-stones，措词简洁而到位。

当然，如果细究，表示时间的"暮"字未译，而在中国古典诗歌当中，此字常见，非常重要，暗含乡愁抑郁之感。不过，译文的亮点，足以掩饰这一缺憾。

总之，相较而言，许渊冲的译文语言稍显平淡，从而导致译诗诗味的单薄；笔者的和 Black 的译文，多有语言上的亮点和妙用，因而译文更具诗味，耐品耐嚼。

（147）夕阳楼（李商隐）

读英文：

I saw her **basking in** the sunshine.

我看到她在阳光下晒太阳。

Premature moves in this respect might well **provoke** a reaction against the reform.

在这方面过早的行动可能会激起对改革的抵触。

Is the **lingering** shadow of the global financial crisis making it harder to accept extravagant indulgences?

全球金融危机所造成的挥之不去的阴影，是否让人们更难接受奢侈放纵？

All enquiries will be dealt with as **speedily** as possible.

所有询问都将从速处理。

They did not know **whither** they should go.

他们不知何去何从。

Listening to his life story **is akin to** reading a good adventure novel.

听他的生活故事就像读一部好的探险小说。

夕阳楼　李商隐 花明柳暗绕天愁， 上尽重城更上楼。 欲问孤鸿向何处， 不知身世自悠悠。	**The Tower Basking in Setting Sun**　Li Shangyin Blooming flowers against dark willows provoke lingering sorrow; atop one after another high tower, again a new tower looms. A solitary goose, in the boundless sky, is soaring speedily, whither? Suddenly I find myself akin to it: witless, aimless, helpless …. （张智中　译）

（148）晓霁（司马光）

读英文：

Spread the bread **thickly** with butter.

把面包抹上厚厚的黄油吧。

Buildings old and new are **thickly** covered with graffiti.

新旧建筑物都覆盖着密密麻麻的涂鸦。

As he pushed it open the voices stilled as though **startled into** silence by the creak of the hinges.

他推开门，那些声音停下了，象是被门的铰链发出的声音震惊得陷入了沉寂。

Don't make a **hurried** decision, look round well first.

别急于做决定，先仔细考虑一下。

I ate a **hurried** breakfast and left.

我匆匆忙忙吃完早饭就离开了。

| 晓霁　司马光

梦觉繁声绝，
林光透隙来。
开门惊乌鸟，
余滴落苍苔。 | **A Fine Morning After the Night Rain**　Sima Guang

Waking up from a nightlong
　　sound sleep, I find thickly
　　　　falling rain let up; wisps
and beams of morning sunshine
　　reach me after penetrating
　　　　forest leaves. Upon my pushing
open the door, crows and
　　magpies are startled into a
　　　　hurried flight, who shake down
from their branches drops
　　of water on the green moss,
　　　　splashing and spattering.
（张智中　译） |

译诗的后面几行，shake down from their branches drops of water on the green moss ...，令人想到美国诗人弗罗斯特一首有名的小诗：

| **Dust of Snow**　Robert Frost

The way a crow
Shook down on me
The dust of snow
From a hemlock tree

Has given my heart
A change of mood
And saves some part
Of a day I had rued. | 雪粉　罗伯特·弗罗斯特

举头望见一只寒
鸦从铁杉枝头散
落雪粉到我身上
的颤颤悠悠模样

一阵突来的惊喜
驱散心头的阴翳
我整日懊丧的心
顿时清亮了几分
（张智中　译） |

需要注意的是，英诗其实是有标点的：最后的句号。这就提醒读者注意，这首诗歌乃一气呵成之作。汉译主要到了这点，用当代流畅之汉语，力图再现

原诗之口吻与意境。诗中，shook down on me …，所绘意境，与司马光《晓霁》有些仿佛，因而，《晓霁》英译之时，仿拟弗罗斯特英文措词与造语。

（149）静夜思（李白）

读英文：

Frosty windows make great surfaces for children to draw on.
有霜的窗户是孩子们画画的好地方。

Her steady **gaze** did not waver.
她目不转睛地注视著。

The compact **disc** is a miracle of modern technology.
激光唱片是当代技术的奇葩。

Mark's eyes **were alight with** excitement.
马克的眼里闪烁着激动的光。

His face **was alight with** anger.
他满脸愠怒的神色。

《静夜思》散译：

Still Night Yearning   Li Bai

The bedside floor is frosty with a beam of moonlight; I lift my gaze

to the disc: my face for home is alight.

分行改为诗体，并回译成汉语：

Still Night Yearning Li Bai	静夜的渴望　李白
The bedside floor is frosty	床边的地上如霜，
with a beam of moonlight;	一道明亮的月光。
I lift my gaze to the disc:	抬眼看向那圆盘，
my face for home is alight.	脸上写满着思乡。
（张智中　译）	（张智中　译）

译诗标题，Still Night Yearning，恰吻合"静夜思"，直译而佳。译文中，系动词 is 加上形容词 frosty，后跟介词 with，是一种常见的富有诗意的表达方式。英文单词 disc，本为"圆盘、盘状物"之意，词典上给出短语：the moon's disc，"月轮"之意。这里，disc 独用，在上下文中，含义也非常清楚了。最后一行：my face for home is alight. 采取了倒装，正常语序是：my face is alight for home. 四行整齐，偶行单词 moonlight 与 alight，押完美韵。回译也诗行整齐划一，尾韵铿锵。可谓格律体译诗。

另外，此诗虽然简单，明白如话，"疑是地上霜"中的"疑是"，如果理解成"怀疑是"，也不算错，例如书上注释："疑是：以为是。疑：怀疑，疑惑。"[102] 但似乎缺少点诗意。最近读到另一本书上的注释："疑是：好像是，简直就是。"[103]感觉这样理解更为合理，至少更加富有诗意。不过，本译采用 is frosty with（"地上如霜"）来表达，避开了这个问题，却同样诗意盎然。

（150）望岳（杜甫）

望岳		
岱宗夫如何？ 齐鲁青未了。 造化钟神秀， 阴阳割昏晓。 荡胸生曾云， 决眦入归鸟。 会当凌绝顶， 一览众山小。	五岳之首的泰山是多么伟大啊！ 在齐鲁两地那青翠的峰峦绵邈。 大自然赋于它全部的神奇和灵秀， 山北山南区别竟同于傍晚和佛晓。 涤荡荡于我胸中的是蒸腾的烟云， 极目才望见一群群归巢的小鸟。 有一天定要登上它最高的山顶， 四下里所有的山丘看来都那么渺小。 （何润香 今译）[104]	呵，泰山，你是多么高大！ 山南山北，一碧无涯。 大自然凝聚着神奇秀异， 阴阳向背竟像有早晚之差。 极目追踪暮归的鸟雀， 胸中涌起重叠的云霞。 我定会登上你的顶峰， 看群山都俯伏在脚下。 （程千帆、徐有富 今译）[105]

显然，两种今译，差别很大，但都达意。不过，也只是散文的释意而已，诗性早已流失殆尽。不能怪译者：诗不可译，这话自有道理。古诗今译，已不可译，况古诗英译乎？

Looking at Tai Mountain

How is grandiose the East High Mountain Tai in the first place?

Its green ranges stretch across two ancient kingdoms to other place.

It's the magical beauty full of great love of the creator,

Dividing dawn and evenfall, shady side and sunny.

The rolling clouds around it stir surging passions in my brain,

102 戴建业，激发孩子想象力的古诗 100 首［M］，上海：复旦大学出版社，2021：177。

103 李均洋，（日）佐藤利行，荣喜朝主编，风月同天：日本人眼中最美中国古诗 100 首［C］，北京：人民文学出版社，2020：19。

104 吴钧陶，汉英对照唐诗三百首［Z］，长沙：湖南出版社，1997：292。

105 人民文学出版社编辑部，唐诗名译［C］，北京：人民文学出版社，2000：63。

I'm staring with fixed eyes at the birds returning to their nests.

I shall surely ascend the summit of the East High Mountain,

Overlooking that those hills get too wee below the mountain.

（刘克璋　译）[106]

标题的英译：Looking at Tai Mountain，两个问题：一方面，Tai Mountain 不是"泰山"的习惯拼法；另一方面，Looking at 不能表达"望岳"之"望"的力度。

首行 How is grandiose the East High Mountain Tai in the first place? 似乎第二和第三个单词的顺序可以调整：How grandiose is the East High Mountain Tai in the first place?

整体观之，译文平淡。

Looking at Mountain Tai

What shall I say about the Mountain Tai?

Further than Qi and Lu its green tracts lie.

The Creator clothes it in divine array;

While its north side shows night, its south side shows day.

With its layers of clouds open hearts rise;

Home-bound birds can be seen with one's strained eyes.

I wish I could climb to its summit someday

And have of smaller mounts a broad survey.

（王玉书　译）[107]

开头的问句，英译为 What shall I say about，显得孱弱无力。"造化"的英文 Creator（造物主），归化过度，非为可取之策。

"荡胸生层云"之英译：With its layers of clouds open hearts rise，似乎难以达意。最后两句，"会当凌绝顶，一览众山小"，乃是名言。英译失去了名言的特质，变成了散文化的平铺直叙。

Gazing at Taishan

What shall I say of the Great Peak?

From here Ch'i and Lu are one unbounded green.

---

106 刘克璋，古诗一百首：汉英对照 [Z]，上海：上海世界图书出版公司，2013：75。
107 王玉书，精选唐诗与唐画（英汉对照）[Z]，北京：五洲传播出版社，2005：14。

Nature for once centred the marvelous:

Its light and shade divide the dawn from dusk.

The clouds in layers sweep my breast;

Into distended sight comes the homing bird.

I must climb up the highest summit,

Contract all mountains in one gaze!

（谢文通　译）[108]

此译显然进步不少：one unbounded green, centred the marvelous, the clouds in layers sweep my breast，into distended sight comes the homing bird，contract all mountains in one gaze 等，这些短语或句子，具有了耐品的味道，虽说离诗味尚有距离。我们觉得，这个译文的水平，大体上等于前引《望岳》两种今译的质量——实属不易。谢文通乃前辈译者，英文功底自佳。来看许渊冲的英译：

Gazing on Mount Tai

O peak of peaks, how high it stands!

One boundless green o'verspreads two States.

A marvel done by Nature's hands,

O'er light and shade it dominates.

Clouds rise therefrom and lave my breast;

My eyes are strained to see birds fleet.

Try to ascend the mountain's crest:

It dwarfs all peaks under our feet.

（许渊冲　译）[109]

译诗将"岱宗"，意即山之鼻祖，英译为 peak of peaks（顶峰中的顶峰），当然巧妙。同一个名词的单数和复数的如此配合，其实在英文语言里普遍运用，在许渊冲的英语译诗中也很常见。但接下来的 how high it stands!（这山多高啊!)，就显得平淡了。

"齐鲁青未了"的英译：One boundless green o'verspreads two States，在不可数名词 green 之前使用 one，似乎欠妥。另外，此句的含义，多用被动来表达。例如高永伟主编的《新英汉词典》上的例子：The sky was overspread with

---

108 谢文通，杜诗选译［Z］，广州：广东高等教育出版社，1985：3。

109 许渊冲，唐诗三百首：汉英对照［Z］，北京：海豚出版社，2013：76。

clouds.（天空布满了云。）如果把这个句子改成主动：Clouds overspread the sky. 似乎感觉不那么自然了。因此，"齐鲁青未了"的英译，似乎采用被动较好：the two states were overspread with green。而译者为什么不这样译呢？显然，是为了让 States 与第四行的 dominates 押韵。另外，把齐鲁淡化译为 two States，本来是可取的策略，但是，首先，States 的首字母似乎无需大写；其次，可以考虑用 kingdoms 来代替 States，更为贴切，因为中国古代之"国"，英文多用 kingdoms。如《三国演义》之英译，就是 The Romance of Three Kingdoms。

"造化钟神秀"的英译：A marvel done by Nature's hands，其中，名词 marvel 似乎不如 wonder，动词 done 似乎不如 wrought，另外，与 States 的首字母无需大写一样，这里的 Nature，同样无需大写。英文大写可以表示强调或拟人，这里似乎没有必要了。

"阴阳割昏晓"的英译：O'er light and shade it dominates（它统治着光和影），表意奇怪而脱离原意。

"荡胸生曾云"的英译，动词 lave（洗涤），措词过实，恐不能表达"荡胸"之"荡"。

"决眦入归鸟"的英译采取被动语态：My eyes are strained to see birds fleet，似乎有外力导致眼睛疲惫，远离了原文的"主观能动性"。另外，英译是 birds fleet（快速奋飞之鸟），而不是"归鸟"。而归鸟在中国古诗中是一个重要的意象，不可轻易改变。

"会当凌绝顶"的英译中，ascend 感觉是自然的上升，不如 climb 或 scale 等词。宾语 the mountain's crest，表述也不太自然，一般说 the crest of the mountain。

"一览众山小"的英译，it dwarfs all peaks（泰山顶峰让其他山峰变成了矮子），意思已经完备，随后的 under our feet，乃是冗余信息，只为 feet 与其上的 fleet 押韵。

整体观之，译诗每行八个音节，押交叉韵。除了韵律工整之外，译诗可取之处不多，虽然许渊冲有其他不错的译诗。接下来，我们看两个西方译者的译文：

Looking at Taishan

Why has Taishan become so

　　sacred?

> See how over Qi and Lu it stands
>
> Never losing its light blue majesty!
>
> Endowed in the beginning with
>
> such
>
> Spirit; its sunny face and then its
>
> darkslopes giving
>
> Dawn and dusk in one moment;
>
> cloud arising
>
> In tiers ever refreshing it; not easy
>
> To follow the birds as they fly
>
> Back up its heights; one day I
>
> shall climb
>
> Clear to the summit,
>
> Seeing how small surrounding
>
> Mountain tops appear as they lie
>
> below me.
>
> （Rewi Alley 路易·艾黎　译）[110]

散体英译中国古诗，是路易·艾黎一以贯之的翻译风格。他的译文，如果散文读之，则是：

> Why has Taishan become so sacred? See how over Qi and Lu it stands: never losing its light blue majesty! Endowed in the beginning with such spirit; its sunny face and then its darkslopes giving dawn and dusk in one moment; cloud arising in tiers ever refreshing it; not easy to follow the birds as they fly back up its heights; one day I shall climb clear to the summit, seeing how small surrounding mountain tops appear as they lie below me.

可谓是一篇不错的散文。把诗歌翻译成散文，我们可能会不屑一顾。且慢——如果我们认真阅读一些古诗英译，特别是中国译者翻译的格律体所谓"忠实"译文之后，我们会觉得很多译诗，其实连散文都算不上的。

---

110 （新西兰）艾黎（Rewi Alley）译，杜甫诗选（汉英对照）[Z]，北京：外文出版社，2001：3。

诗不可译，是指诗歌，不可译为诗歌；但如果退而求其次，译为散文，大概还是可以的。而且，如果机缘巧合，一篇好的散文，是完全可以顶得上一首诗歌的。

Gazing at the Great Mount

To what shall I compare

The Sacred Mount that stands,

A balk of green that hath no end,

Betwixt two lands!

Nature did fuse and blend

All mystic beauty there,

Where Dark and Light

Do dusk and dawn unite.

Gazing, soul-cleansed, at Thee

From clouds upsprung, one may

Mark with wide eyes the homing flight

Of birds. Some day

Must I thy topmost height

Mount, at one glance to see

Hills numberless

Dwindle to nothingness.

（John Turner 唐安石　译）[111]

散文读之：

To what shall I compare the Sacred Mount that stands, a balk of green that hath no end, betwixt two lands! Nature did fuse and blend all mystic beauty there, where Dark and Light do dusk and dawn unite. Gazing, soul-cleansed, at Thee from clouds upsprung, one may mark with wide eyes the homing flight of birds. Some day must I thy topmost height mount, at one glance to see hills numberless dwindle to nothingness.

是的，没错，就是散文。耐人品味的散文。我们再冷静反思一下：林语堂、

---

111 王峰、马琰，唐诗英译集注、比录、鉴评与索引 [C]，西安：陕西人民出版社，2011：135-136。

杨宪益以降，有几个中国译者能译出漂亮的一流的英文散文？汉语散文的英译，真正成功者，又有几人？如果散文的汉译英尚不能成功，岂可在诗歌的汉译英方面得意洋洋踌躇满志呢？

Gazing Up at T'ai Mountain

How becomes the T'ai a worshipful mountain? See how the greenness of the surrounding plains is never lost. Creation has lavished there its mysterious wonders; The sunny and shady sides fashion dawn and dusk at the same moment.

The growing layers of clouds might scour one's bosom of worldly thoughts; To follow those returning birds would strain my eyes. One day I shall climb like Confucius to the top To see how the surrounding hills dwarf into moles.

（William Hung 洪业　译）

洪业的译文，采取真正的散文体，只是将译文分成两段，如此而已。不过，行中偶然采取单词首字母大写，似乎在暗示这是诗行的开头：这表明译者并没有与诗体译文彻底决裂。另外，译文中的 Creation，仍属西化；like Confucius 的添加，虽然正确，却无必要，毕竟诗歌重在抒情。同时，lavish，fashion（使成形；塑造）和短语 scour one's bosom of worldly thoughts 的使用，乃译文的出彩之处；shall 一词，正表决心。整体观之，译文不逊于上引 Rewi Alley 和 John Turner 的译文。

此译选自美国哈佛大学出版社 1952 年出版的 *Tu Fu: China's Greatest Poet*，作者洪业，正是靠散文英译古诗而闻名的译家。根据网上资料：William Hung，中文名字洪业（1893－1980），福建侯官人。现代著名史学家、教育家。先后就读于卫斯良大学、哥伦比亚大学、纽约协和神学院，获得文学学士、文学硕士、神学学士等学位。1923 年回国，被聘为燕京大学历史系教授，任大学文理科科长，先后兼任历史系主任、大学图书馆馆长、研究院文科主任及导师等。创办《燕京学报》，并以哈佛—燕京学社引得编纂处主任总纂哈佛—燕京学社《引得》64 种。1946 年春赴美讲学，1948 至 1968 年兼任哈佛大学东亚系研究员。1980 年在美国去世。其学术名篇有《考利玛窦之世界地图》、《礼记引得序》、《春秋经传引得序》、《杜诗引得序》、《〈蒙古秘史〉源流考》、《破斧》等。所撰《礼记引得序》于 1937 年获法国巴黎茹理安（一作儒莲）奖金。主要著述见《洪业论学集》（北京：中华书局，1981 年）、Tu Fu: China's Greatest Poet（美国哈佛大学出版社，1952 年）。

译者有这样的经历，英文修养便不比西方译者差，所以译文在美国受到读者欢迎。再来看霍克斯（David Hawkes）的散体译文：

On a Prospect of T'ai-shan

How is one to describe this king of mountains? Throughout the whole of Ch'i and Lu one never loses sight of its greenness. In it the Creator has concentrated all that is numinous and beautiful. Its northern and southern slopes divide the dawn from the dark. The layered clouds begin at the climber's heaving chest, and homing birds fly suddenly within range of his straining eyes. One day I must stand on top of its highest peak and at a single glance see all the other mountains grown tiny beneath me.

（David Hawkes 霍克斯　译）

因为英译《红楼梦》，霍克斯鼎鼎大名于中外。但是，但是，就此诗的英译而言，看不出比洪业、Rewi Alley 或 John Turner 高明多少。原诗第三行的英译中，numinous 一词稍偏，"超自然的；神圣的；令人肃然起敬的"之意。最后，"会当凌绝顶，一览众山小"的英译：I must stand on top of its highest peak and at a single glance see all the other mountains grown tiny beneath me，力气屡弱。似乎译者没有充分理解这句话背后的决心与决意。再看宇文所安的译文：

Gazing on the Peak

And what then is Daizong like? ——

over Qi and Lu, green unending.

Creation compacted spirit splendors here,

Dark and Light, riving dusk and dawn.

Exhilirating the breast, it produces layers of cloud;

Splitting eye-pupils, it has homing birds entering.

Someday may I climb up to its highest summit,

with one sweeping view see how small all other mountains are.

（Stephen Owen 宇文所安　译）[112]

---

112 Owen, Stephen. The Poetry of Du Fu. Boston/Berlin: Walter de Gruyter Inc., 2016: 3.

音译的 Daizong，实在是无甚意义。第二行中的 Qi 和 Lu，在没有解释没有着落的情况下，英语读者也会摸不着头脑，不知其所云。Creation 仍属归化，以西方文化来阐释中国古诗，不足可取。第五行第一个单词 Exhilirating，应该是 Exhilarating 的误拼。接下来，"决眦入归鸟"之"决眦"，英译 splitting eye-pupils，用力过猛：或许英语读者真以为眼睛瞪坏了呢。最后两行中，may 的措词，以及整个句式的布局，都未能译出原诗的决心和气势。宇文所安断言：中国古诗决不能让中国译者来译。但他自己译了，也不过如此。辛顿（David Hinton）的译文：

Gazing at the Sacred Peak

What is this ancestor Exalt Mountain like?

Endless greens of north and south meeting

where Changemaker distills divine beauty,

where *yin* and *yang* cleave dusk and dawn.

Chest heaving breathes out cloud, and eyes

open dusk bird-flight home. One day soon,

on the summit, peaks ranging away will be

small enough to hold, all in a single glance.

（David Hinton 辛顿 译）[113]

诗歌虽然不押尾韵，却是整齐的豆腐块，令人想起一个多世纪之前闻一多青睐的诗歌形式。将"岱宗"意译为 Exalt Mountain，其中，Exalt 为"赞扬；提升；加强"之意。虽然地理意义上不太明确，但在诗歌里却能带来美感，这就足够了。接下来，"齐鲁青未了"中的"齐鲁"，在译文中淡化为南北（north and south），正如专名"岱宗"的淡化处理一样，在诗歌里都是化繁为简的手法。然后，与"造化钟神秀"的英译，合并一起：Endless greens of north and south meeting where Changemaker distills divine beauty，从而发挥了英文的优势。"造化"，用 Changemaker，可谓大嘉；distills（蒸馏；提炼）也非原文"钟"的"聚集"之意，但却非常有诗意，而且意思没有走偏太多，令人耳目一新。另外，译者运用了英文的跨行优势，例如，One day soon 应该是下一行的内容，被提到上一行了。

同时，"决眦入归鸟"的英译：and eyes open dusk bird-flight home；"荡胸

---

113 陈琳，欣顿与山水诗的生态话语性［Z］，杭州：浙江大学出版社，2019：184。

生层云"的英译：Chest heaving breathes out cloud，显然是过于直译的结果。"会当凌绝顶"中的动词"凌"字，没有译出，显有损失。另外一个重要的理解问题，就是"阴阳割昏晓"的英译：where *yin* and *yang* cleave dusk and dawn。这里的音译，暗示了译者对原文的误解。对应的今译，分别是"山北山南区别竟同于傍晚和佛晓"和"阴阳向背竟像有早晚之差"。杜甫这里的"阴阳"，不是道家哲学里的阴阳，而是"山北山南"或"阴阳向背"之意，因此不能音译。外国译者的短板，往往在此，虽然辛顿已经精通中国的老庄哲学。

总之，辛顿"对原诗中的每一言的字面意义都予以了翻译，但又是以现代英语诗学的特征表现出来。"[114]这是他译文的风格和优点。同时，他的局限性，也是显然可见的。

在研读以上译文，并经过长期英文阅读之后，笔者给出如下散体译文：

Gazing on Mount Tai

What a striking spectacle does Mount Tai exhibit! The kingdoms of northward Qi and southward Lu assume volumes of fresh verdure which stretch over the mountain endlessly. The great nature graces it with a boundless beauty which is a wonder: sacred and splendid; when the northward aspect is shady like dusk, the southward aspect is sunny like dawn, each its own moments: a distinct display of sunshine and shade by nature's magical might which no writing can portray. A welcome thought: clouds upon clouds bring a renewal of hope and a reviving of spirits, even produce a refreshing feeling of exhilaration in me; I fix my strained eyes upon the homing birds with a look which is sharp, focused, and steady. Someday I'll scale the height of the heights of the high mountain with unabated vigour, neither weary of adventure, nor willing to relax my efforts; before taking a little refreshment, I'll have it in my power to enjoy the enclosing fair hills about me — the miniature landscape under my feet.

（张智中　译）

汉语回译如下：

---

114 陈琳，欣顿与山水诗的生态话语性［Z］，杭州：浙江大学出版社，2019：180。

望泰山

泰山之景，给人印象何其深刻！北面的齐国和南面的鲁国，峰峦青翠而绵邈，一碧而无涯。大自然钟灵集秀，叹无边之美景：烂漫，神圣。当北面山坡像黄昏一样黯淡之时，南面山坡却早晨般阳光灿烂，时态各异：大自然是魔术师，在清晰地演绎着光与影的变幻——非笔墨所能尽描。此思此想，多么令人愉快：层层的云彩，带来萌生的希望和重振的精神，甚至在我内心产生了阵阵兴奋的感觉；我瞪着眼睛，使劲盯着归飞的鸟儿，目光锋利、稳定、聚焦。有朝一日，我定要登上那高高的泰山顶峰中的顶峰，抖擞着精神，既不倦于猎奇，也不丝毫懈怠；在驻足休息之前，我就能欣赏到脚下秀丽的群山——脚下的盆景。

（张智中　译）

如果不计标题而计标点的话，杜甫原诗共 48 个字，英译的回译，竟然多达 269 字——译文翻了 5 倍多。这是否太夸张了呢？是否随便添加随意创造任性发挥了呢？仔细品来，却无一点不是来自原文，都是原文的诗性想象和诗性发挥，因而都在合理的范围之内。我们不妨说，原文是一首精炼的古诗，译文则是一篇酣畅淋漓的散文——带着浓浓的诗性。

其实，如此英语译文，多是阅读英文的结果。下面我们逐句分析。

译文首句 What a striking spectacle does Mount Tai exhibit!

其中的名词 spectacle（景象；场面；奇观），一般译者不会想起来。根据《新英汉词典》对 spectacle 的解释，"演出"之外，还有"景象，奇观，引人好奇的人或事物"等意思。例如：a charming spectacle: 赏心悦目的情景。

其实，首句英译来自一句英文：

Without a woman to rule him and think for him, he is a truly lamentable **spectacle**: a baby with whiskers.

没有女人的控制，没有女人为他考虑事情，他就是一个真正可怜、不幸的人：一个长着胡须的婴儿。

从汉语译文来看，看不出 spectacle 的痕迹，其实，已经暗含在字里行间了，这似乎恰恰说明这个词语用得巧妙。反观"岱宗夫如何？"字面上也没有"景象；场面；奇观"，但却暗含此意，因此，用之而佳。再看李白《望庐山瀑布》及其英译：

望庐山瀑布　李白 日照香炉生紫烟， 遥看瀑布挂前川。 飞流直下三千尺， 疑是银河落九天。	**Behold, Lushan Cataract!**　Li Bai The purple mist ascending from the Incense Burner solar-lit, Behold! Yonder hangs a cataract over the river pouring from the Summit. Plump dives a three-thousand-chi outpouring on the fly, What a spectacle, the very picture of a galaxy descending from the empyrean sky! （黄龙　译）[115]

最后一行英译，所添加的 What a spectacle，正是译文的亮点。一般译者也想不起来使用这个单词。

霍克斯英译《红楼梦》第十六回中，也有 spectacle 的妙用：

谁家有那些钱买这个虚热闹去！

No family that ever lived had money enough of its own to pay for such spectacles of vanity!

再回首，《望岳》开篇"岱宗夫如何？"，英译不难：What about Mount Tai? 但这只是译意，而非译诗。开篇一问，随后便是对此一问题的回答和具体描写——泰山恢弘壮观之景。如此之景，当然可用如上之 spectacle。

那么，稍作思考，"岱宗夫如何？"英译如下：

What a striking spectacle does Mount Tai exhibit!

又读英文：

There was the sea; its green volume brought despair.

我仍然记得海洋；它绿色的体积使得我们绝望。[116]

高永伟主编《新英汉词典》对 volume 的第四条解释："大量，许多：a great volume of water 大量水"；陆谷孙主编《英汉大词典》对 volume 的第四条解释："大量，许多；（烟、蒸汽等的）大团：a volume of mail 大批邮件；volumes of black smoke 大团大团的黑烟。"

由此可见，在李立扬的英文诗里，volume 是个巧妙的措词，而相应的汉译，却只是望文生义，没能抓住这一词语的内在精髓。李立扬英文名 Li-Young Lee，1957 年生于印度尼西亚，1964 年随全家移居美国。李立扬的母亲是袁世

---

115 杨洋，古意新声：初级本 [C]，武汉：湖北教育出版社，2002：47。

116 （美）李立扬著；周筱静译，在我爱你的这座城：汉英对照 [M]，北京：知识产权出版社，2016：42-43。

凯的孙女，其父亲李国源曾做过毛泽东主席的私人随从。李立扬是美国最具影响力的当代诗人之一，其诗歌多次获奖，有诗作被选入《牛津当代美国诗选》《诺顿现代诗选》《西斯美国文学选》等权威选本。因此，他的英文诗集《在我爱你的这座城》（The City in Which I Love You）措词肯定没有问题，只是读者或译者的理解问题了。这里，若借用杜甫之诗句，似可译为："这就是那海洋：其青，青未了，带来绝望。"不过，我们的重点，不在英译汉，而在汉译英之英文原创语言精华之吸取和运用。

那么，李立扬的英文 green volume，应该可以联想到杜甫《望岳》第二行"齐鲁青未了"的英译。又，最近读到勃朗特三姐妹中的小妹安妮·勃朗特（Anne Bronte）的带有自传性质的小说《阿格尼丝·格雷》（Agnes Grey），其中有这么一个句子：

> And the graceful deer browsing on its moist herbage already assuming the freshness and verdure of spring.
> 姿态优雅的鹿正在舔食早已呈现出春日的清新和青翠的湿草。

这个描写翠绿的句子，似乎也可借用。不过，外语教学与研究出版社出版的日本学者市川繁治郎主编的《英语搭配大辞典》里，有 fresh verdure of spring 的例子。因此，可以考虑将原文 the freshness and verdure of...的并列关系，改为 fresh verdure 的偏正关系。

关于"齐鲁青未了"：春秋时，齐国在泰山之北，鲁国在泰山之南。后泛指山东一带为齐鲁。青：指泰山青翠的山色。未了：不尽，无穷无尽之意。

因此，"齐鲁青未了"似可如此英译：

The kingdoms of northward Qi and southward Lu assume volumes of fresh verdure which stretch over the mountain endlessly.

如此，正对应今译"在齐鲁两地那青翠的峰峦绵邈"，或"山南山北，一碧无涯"。

第二句呈现的是一片翠绿的景色。那么，回头来译第一句"岱宗夫如何？"似乎当如此表述：**What a striking spectacle does Mount Tai exhibit!** 这样，可在语气上对应"五岳之首的泰山是多么伟大啊！"或"呵，泰山，你是多么高大！"之喟叹。

在"造化钟神秀"中，造化，指大自然；钟，聚集之意。英译：

The great nature graces it with a boundless beauty which is a

wonder: sacred and splendid.

此句英译中，great，nature，graces，sacred 四个单词押元音韵；great 与 graces，boundless 与 beauty，with，which 与 wonder，sacred 与 splendid，分别押头韵；nature 与 wonder，graces 与 boundless，sacred 与 splendid，分别押单词尾韵。其中 sacred 与 splendid 既押头韵又押尾韵。于是，句子耐品耐味，堪与今译媲美："大自然赋于它全部的神奇和灵秀"或"大自然凝聚着神奇秀异"。

"阴阳割昏晓"：阴：山北为阴，即山之背阴面。阳：山南为阳，即山之向阳面。割：分割。昏晓：山北背日故曰昏，山南向日故曰晓。

读英文：

> My employments were too numerous, my leisure **moments** too precious, to admit of much time being given to fruitless lamentations.
>
> 我的工作太多，空闲时间太宝贵了，不允许我把很多时间用于无益的悲伤。
>
> I had to spend a considerable portion of my valuable leisure **moments** on my knees upon the floor, in painfully reducing things to order.
>
> 我只得花去一大部分宝贵的业余时间，跪在地板上，煞费苦心地把房间整理干净。

可见，英文单词 moments，可用来表示"阴阳割昏晓"中所暗示的天光云影之变幻。此句英译：

When the northward aspect is shady like dusk, the southward aspect is sunny like dawn, each its own moments: a distinct display of sunshine and shade by nature's magical might.

回译汉语：

> 当北面山坡像黄昏一样黯淡之时，南面山坡却早晨般阳光灿烂，
>
> 时态各异：大自然是魔术师，在清晰地演绎着光与影的变幻。

相比于今译的"山北山南区别竟同于傍晚和佛晓"或"阴阳向背竟像有早晚之差"，英译丰厚多了。这里，译者发挥自己的想象，但却是在原诗基础之上的发挥，是中国古典诗歌的当代"阐释"，所谓从心所欲，而不逾矩。

诗歌开篇："岱宗夫如何？"诗人用三个句子来进行描述：从"齐鲁青未了"到"造化钟神秀"到"阴阳割昏晓"。其实，泰山的宏伟景观和恢弘气势，

非笔墨所能尽描。于是，读到下面的英文句子：

... followed by an account of her pious resignation, delivered in the usual emphatic, declamatory style, **which no writing can portray**.

接着又讲述她对上帝的虔诚和顺从，说话时用的还是她习惯的那种夸张的语气和雄辩的姿态，简直非笔墨所能形容。

便觉得 which no writing can portray 可用。因此，似乎可在"阴阳割昏晓"的英译之后，加上此语：

When the northward aspect is shady like dusk, the southward aspect is sunny like dawn, each its own moments: a distinct display of sunshine and shade by nature's magical might which no writing can portray.

描景之后，诗人接着抒情："荡胸生曾云"。"曾云"，即"层云"，或"蒸腾的烟云"；意为山中云气吞吐，涤荡胸襟。其实，这里暗含着作者望岳之时的心灵震撼，当然就有着强烈的激动心情。以下英文句子可资借用：

But the morning **brought a renewal of hope and spirits**.

然而，清晨又带来希望，精神也重新振作起来。

As we drove along, **my spirits revived again**.

随着车马的前行，我的精神重新振作起来。

这两个英文句子中的 a renewal of hope and spirits 和 my spirits revived，正可表示振作精神。

再看如下英文句子：

It was truly **refreshing** to hear such a sermon, after being so long accustomed to the dry, prosy discourses of the former curate, and the still less edifying harangues of the rector.

长期以来我听惯了前人副牧师干巴乏味的讲道以及教区长那更缺乏教育意义的夸夸其谈，现在听到这样一次布道真使我精神为之一振。

I rose next morning **with a feeling of hopeful exhilaration**, in spite of the disappointment already experienced.

尽管已有了令人失望的经验，第二天早晨起床时，我心头又涌起强烈的憧憬。

在上引的两个英文句子中，refreshing 和 a feeling of hopeful exhilaration，也可表示"精神一振"或"心头涌起强烈的憧憬"。

那么，"荡胸生曾云"可尝试英译如下：

Clouds upon clouds bring a renewal of hope and a reviving of spirits, even produce a refreshing feeling of exhilaration in me.

回译汉语："层层的云彩，带来萌生的希望和重振的精神，甚至在我内心产生了阵阵兴奋的感觉。"

比较两种今译："涤荡于我胸中的是蒸腾的烟云"和"胸中涌起重叠的云霞"，可知英译更为洒脱自由，离形得似，仿佛诗人之情怀。

又读到如下英文句子：

And this was an unwelcome thought.

我不喜欢这样的想法。

当然，否定句可改成肯定句：And this was a welcome thought. 其实，welcome 作形容词，按照《新英汉词典》的解释，可以表示"可喜的，令人愉快的"。例如：welcome news 好消息；a welcome opportunity 好机会。

在《望岳》中，既然诗人从"荡胸生曾云"开始抒情，写心中所想。那么，不妨在此加上一个过渡，或可起到引领之作用。此谓增译之法。那么，再回首，**"荡胸生曾云"**英译如下：

A welcome thought: clouds upon clouds bring a renewal of hope and a reviving of spirits, even produce a refreshing feeling of exhilaration in me.

在"决眦入归鸟"中，"决眦"，意即睁大眼睛；"决"，裂开，"眦"，眼眶。两种今译："极目才望见一群群归巢的小鸟"，"极目追踪暮归的鸟雀"。可见泰山之险峻高远旷邈。读下面英文句子：

And **fixing her cold, stony eyes upon me with a look** that could not be mistaken, she would shut the door, and walk away.

她那冷酷无情的目光盯住我看了一会儿，其中的含义不容误解，然后她关上门就走开了。

Harold stared ahead, **straining** to find a sense of direction, or the break in the cloud that had so delighted him, but it was like looking at the world through net curtains again.

哈罗德望着前方，努力寻找一点方向感，或是乌云间透出的一丝光亮，但感觉就像是隔着家里厚厚的窗帘企望看见外面的世界一样。

当然可以借用。"决眦入归鸟"英译如下：

I fix my strained eyes upon the homing birds with a look which is sharp, focused, and steady.

回译汉语：

我瞪着眼睛，使劲盯着归飞的鸟儿，目光锋利、稳定、聚焦。

显然，英译用词形象传神。

"会当凌绝顶"：会当，终将，定要。凌，登上。绝顶，即泰山的最高峰。英文阅读：

I returned, however, **with unabated vigour** to my work.
然而，我还是精神饱满地回去工作了。

I was not yet weary of adventure, **nor willing to relax my efforts**.
但我的冒险精神没有并没有消沉，我不愿放弃努力。

这里的 with unabated vigour，"精神饱满"，或精力没有丝毫衰退之意。如此而登泰山，正是杜甫之精气神也。而 not yet weary of adventure 和 nor willing to relax my efforts，可表示诗人不登山顶誓不罢休之决绝意志。其中的 adventure，不一定非要表示一般意义上的"冒险"，也可以是《新英汉词典》里的第三个含义："激动人心或异乎寻常的经历"。

"会当凌绝顶"尝试英译：

Someday I'll scale the height of the heights of the high mountain with unabated vigour, neither weary of adventure, nor willing to relax my efforts.

《新英汉词典》中 scale 词条的例子：scale new heights of science and technology 攀登科学技术新高峰。译文变通为 the height of heights（顶峰中的顶峰），更符合泰山峰峦叠嶂之绵延状貌。随后再启用 high，只为带来三个元音重叠之音韵效果。增译部分，平行阅读之英文 not yet ... nor ...，改为 neither ... nor ...，更符合当代英文用法。勃朗特的小说出版于 1847，距今已有 170 余年之久。

英译之汉语回译：

有朝一日，我定要登上那高高的泰山顶峰中的顶峰，抖擞着精神，既不倦于猎奇，也不丝毫懈怠。

反观"会当凌绝顶"的两种今译："有一天定要登上它最高的山顶"；"我定会登上你的顶峰"，可知英译注入了译者充沛的情感——这种情感，正是译者体会到的诗人杜甫的情感。

"一览众山小"，此句出自《孟子·尽心上》"登泰山小天下"，这是孔子的理想。如果说"会当凌绝顶"表示诗人决心之大，最后一句"一览众山小"，却表示诗人气势之盛——泰山之恢弘伟岸，即诗人之心胸阔大。因此，今译一，"四下里所有的山丘看来都那么渺小"，似乎不如今译二更有气势："看群山都俯伏在脚下"。

译诗，非译字，译其内涵，译其气势，译其境界也。至于英译，却要看异域语言的姻缘巧合，方知译文能否成功。

"一览众山小"之平行英文阅读：

With due politeness, however, she showed me my bedroom, and left me there **to take a little refreshment**.

不过，她还是以应有的礼貌带我去看了我的卧室，把我独自留下休息了一会儿。

I was glad **I had it in my power to** cheer him by my return, and to amuse him with singing his favourite songs.

我高兴的是，我的归来能给他带来欢乐，我还为他唱他喜爱的歌曲，使他快慰。

其中，to take a little refreshment（休息一会儿），似可反其意而用之，表示"一刻也不休息"——当然，这是上句"会当凌绝顶"的语义接续。如果补而充之，似乎亦可。

第二个英文句子中的 I had it in my power to ...，"我能……"之意，语气微妙而佳，可谓无往而不婉转，需读者深刻，才能体而会之。

另，登顶之后，"一览众山小"，眼中所"览"之景，若联想到公园里常见之"盆景"miniature landscape，当为妙词。

好了，"一览众山小"尝试英译：

Before taking a little refreshment, I'll have it in my power to enjoy the enclosing fair hills about me — the miniature landscape

under my feet.

回译汉语：

在驻足休息之前，我就能欣赏到脚下的群山——脚下的盆景。

再回头比读两种今译："四下里所有的山丘看来都那么渺小"；"看群山都俯伏在脚下"，可知英译有了暗喻——这或许就是所谓译者的灵感闪现所致，因而出彩。

总之，《望岳》由望岳而生登临之想，通过描写泰山恢弘壮观之景，表达了诗人昂扬向上，欲攀登泰山之绝顶而俯视一切的豪情，表现了青年杜甫积极进取、壮志凌云的气概和抱负。

《望岳》之英译，如果我们的译文止步于之前的散文翻译，也是可以的，正如上引霍克斯和洪业等人的译文一样。但是，在灵感之下，我们还是把杜甫《望岳》的英译及其回译，做了诗歌形式的排列：

Gazing on Mount Tai Du Fu

What

a striking spectacle

does Mount Tai exhibit!

The kingdoms of northward Qi

and southward Lu assume volumes

of fresh verdure which stretch over the mountain

endlessly. The great nature graces it with a boundless beauty

which is a wonder: sacred and splendid; when the northward aspect

is shady like dusk, the southward aspect is sunny like dawn, each

its own

moments: a distinct display of sunshine and shade by nature's

magical might

which no writing can portray. A welcome thought: clouds upon

clouds bring a renewal

of hope and a reviving of spirits, even produce a refreshing feeling

of exhilaration in me;

I fix my strained eyes upon the homing birds with a look which is

sharp, focused, and steady.

Someday I'll scale the height of the heights of the high mountain

with unabated vigour, neither

weary of adventure, nor willing to relax my efforts; before taking a

little refreshment, I'll have it

in my power to enjoy the enclosing fair hills about me — the

miniature landscape under my feet.

（张智中　译）

望泰山　杜甫

泰山

之景，给人

印象何其深刻！

北面的齐国和南面

的鲁国，峰峦青翠而绵

邈，一碧而无涯。大自然钟

灵集秀，叹无边之美景：烂漫，神

圣。当北面山坡像黄昏一样黯淡之时，

南面山坡却早晨般阳光灿烂，时态各异：

大自然是魔术师，在清晰地演绎着光与影的

变幻——非笔墨所能尽描。此思此想，多么令人

愉快：层层的云彩，带来萌生的希望和重振的精神，

甚至在我内心产生了阵阵兴奋的感觉；我瞪着眼睛，使劲

盯着归飞的鸟儿，目光锋利、稳定、聚焦。有朝一日，我定要

登上那高高的泰山顶峰中的顶峰，抖擞着精神，既不倦于猎

奇，也不

丝毫懈怠；在驻足休息之前，我就能欣赏到脚下秀丽的群山—

—脚下的盆景。

（张智中　译）

显然，这就是新诗里常见的图形诗了。这——不正是泰山的形状吗？巍巍乎高哉！

"翻译的挑战，首先在于在中国文学对外译介中究竟如何选择恰当的翻

译方法。"[117]"翻译的挑战，其次在于在中国文学对外译介中究竟如何树立正确的翻译观念。……葛浩文的翻译是否能够被视为忠实性翻译的绝对对立面？试问，倘若'忠实于原文'的翻译理念果真已经成为阻碍中国文学对外译介与传播的'绊脚石'，那么，取而代之的又该是怎样的翻译标准与翻译原则？"[118]在莫言获奖的初期，作为莫言的首席翻译，葛浩文却没有得到中国翻译界的掌声与致谢，反倒被认为是译文不忠、连改带编的"千古罪人"。近年来，中国学界开始反思，似乎对葛浩文的翻译理念有所思考、有所接受。

在古诗英译方面，无论中国译者还是西方译者，都缺乏葛浩文式的翻译，即译文太过讲求忠实而走向拘泥，甚至到拘泥不化的地步。可以说，照字面翻译，讲究文字的忠实——似乎是西方译者的共性；而中国译者的共性，一般是讲究押韵，追求韵律上的忠实。这两种做法，似乎都背离了诗之为诗的本质。文字也好，韵律也好，都是为"诗"服务的。在诗歌不能译的情况下，译者更应该集中精力于译"诗"，而不是译文字和译格律。要之，译诗——就是翻译诗，不是翻译文字，也不是翻译格律或韵律。

通过对杜甫《望岳》多个译文的比读，通过我们对英文阅读的吸收和对原诗诗意的阐释，我们走向了阐释性的或解构性的翻译，这似乎是葛浩文的翻译理念在古诗英译中的运用。我们觉得，这样的译文，虽然不同于传统意义上的古诗英译，也是中国古诗英译的一种努力，或许有望迎来灿烂的明天。

总之，作为汉诗英译的译者，无论中外，都必须大量阅读英文，汲取英文精华，并善加运用，只有这样，才能切实提高译文的质量和水平，为中国诗歌走向英语世界做出贡献。

---

117 刘云虹，翻译批评研究 [M]，南京：南京大学出版社，2015：291。
118 刘云虹，翻译批评研究 [M]，南京：南京大学出版社，2015：292。

参考文献

1. 陈君朴，汉英对照唐诗绝句 150 首［Z］，上海：上海大学出版社，2005。

2. 陈琳，欣顿与山水诗的生态话语性［Z］，杭州：浙江大学出版社，2019。

3. 陈煜斓，语堂智慧智慧语堂［C］，福州：福建教育出版社，2016。

4. 戴建业，激发孩子想象力的古诗 100 首［M］，上海：复旦大学出版社，
   2021。

5. 都森、陈玉筠，古韵新声——唐诗绝句 108 首（英汉对照）［Z］，武汉：
   华中科技大学出版社，2011。

6. 冯志杰，唐诗绝句 100 首［Z］，北京：当代中国出版社，2019。

7. 龚景浩，英译唐诗名作选［Z］，北京：商务印书馆，2006。

8. 郭著章等，唐诗精品百首英译（修订版）［Z］，武汉：武汉大学出版社，
   2010。

9. 华满元、华先发，汉诗英译名篇选读［C］，武汉：武汉大学出版社，2014。

10. 黄遵洸，英诗咀华［M］，杭州：浙江工商大学出版社，2014。

11. 江岚，唐诗西传史论——以唐诗在英美的传播为中心［M］，北京：学苑
    出版社，2009。

12. 黎昌抱，王佐良翻译风格研究［M］，北京：光明日报出版社，2009。

13. 李均洋，（日）佐藤利行，荣喜朝主编，风月同天：日本人眼中最美中国
    古诗 100 首［C］，北京：人民文学出版社，2020。

14. （美）李立扬著；周筱静译，在我爱你的这座城：汉英对照［M］，北京：
    知识产权出版社，2016。

15. 李运兴，英译中国名家散文选：汉英对照［Z］，上海：上海外语教育出版社，2019。

16. 刘克璋，古诗一百首：汉英对照［Z］，上海：上海世界图书出版公司，2013。

17. 刘文杰，英语诗歌汉译与赏析［Z］，广州：中山大学出版社，2014。

18. 刘云虹，翻译批评研究［M］，南京：南京大学出版社，2015。

19. 刘云虹，葛浩文翻译研究［C］，南京：南京大学出版社，2019。

20. 鲁迅著，（英）詹纳尔（W. J. F. Jenner）译，鲁迅诗选：汉英对照［Z］，北京：外文出版社，2016。

21. 洛夫，唐诗解构［M］，南京：江苏凤凰文艺出版社，2015。

22. 裘小龙，汉英对照中国古典爱情诗词选［Z］，上海：上海社会科学院出版社，2003。

23. 人民文学出版社编辑部，唐诗名译［C］，北京：人民文学出版社，2000。

24. 任治稷、余正，从诗到诗：中国古诗词英译［Z］，北京：外语教学与研究出版社，2006。

25. 沈庆利，写在心灵边上：中外抒情诗歌欣赏［M］，北京：中国纺织出版社，2001。

26. 束慧娟，基于意义进化论的典籍英译模式研究［M］，苏州：苏州大学出版社，2019。

27. 孙大雨，英译唐诗选：汉英对照［Z］，上海：上海外语教育出版社，2007。

28. 孙会军，葛浩文和他的中国文学译介［M］，上海：上海交通大学出版社，2016。

29. 孙宜学，中华文化国际传播：途径与方法创新［M］，上海：同济大学出版社，2016。

30. 汤富华，翻译的诗学批评［M］，南京：南京大学出版社，2019。

31. 陶友兰、强晓，本科翻译专业阅读教学综合模式探讨［J］，中国翻译，2015，(1)。

32. 王大濂，英译唐诗绝句百首［Z］，天津：百花文艺出版社，1997。

33. 王峰、马琰，唐诗英译集注、比录、鉴评与索引［C］，西安：陕西人民出版社，2011。

34. 王宏，基于"大中华文库"的中国典籍英译翻译策略研究［M］，杭州：浙江大学出版社，2019。

35. 王家新，在一颗名叫哈姆雷特的星下［M］，北京：中国人民大学出版社，2012。

36. 王玉书，精选唐诗与唐画（汉英对照）［Z］，北京：五洲传播出版社，2005。

37. 汪榕培、任秀桦，诗经：中英文版［Z］，沈阳：辽宁教育出版社，1995。

38. 文殊、王晋熙、邓炎昌，唐宋绝句名篇英译［Z］，北京：外语教学与研究出版社，1995。

39. 翁显良，古诗英译［Z］，北京：北京出版社，1985。

40. 吴钧陶，汉英对照唐诗三百首［Z］，长沙：湖南出版社，1997。

41. 谢韩，讲给孩子的唐宋诗［M］，成都：四川人民出版社，2019。

42. 谢文通，杜诗选译［Z］，广州：广东高等教育出版社，1985。

43. （新西兰）艾黎（Rewi Alley），杜甫诗选（汉英对照）［Z］，北京：外文出版社，2001。

44. 邢全臣，用英语欣赏国粹：英汉对照［Z］，北京：科学出版社，2008。

45. 徐晓飞、房国铮，翻译与文化：翻译中的文化建构［M］，上海：上海交通大学出版社，2019。

46. 许渊冲，汉英对照宋词三百首［Z］，北京：高等教育出版社，2004。

47. 许渊冲，精选毛泽东诗词与诗意画［Z］，北京：五洲传播出版社，2006。

48. 许渊冲，李白诗选：汉英对照［Z］，长沙：湖南人民出版社，2007。

49. 许渊冲，诗经（汉英对照）［Z］，长沙：湖南出版社，1993。

50. 许渊冲，宋词三百首：汉英对照［Z］，北京：海豚出版社，2013。

51. 许渊冲，宋元明清诗选：汉英对照［Z］，北京：海豚出版社，2013。

52. 许渊冲，唐诗三百首：汉英对照［Z］，北京：海豚出版社，2013。

53. 许渊冲，唐宋诗一百五十首：汉英对照［Z］，北京：北京大学出版社，1995。

54. 许渊冲，唐五代词选：汉英对照［Z］，北京：海豚出版社，2013。

55. 许渊冲，新编千家诗［Z］，北京：中华书局，2006。

56. 许渊冲，许渊冲译千家诗：汉文、英文［Z］，北京：中译出版社，2021。

57. 许渊冲，许渊冲英译李白诗选：汉英对照［Z］，北京：中国对外翻译出版有限公司，2014。

58. 晏榕，诗的复活：诗意现实的现代构成与新诗学——美国现当代诗歌论衡及引申［M］，杭州：浙江大学出版社，2013。

59. 杨洋，古意新声：初级本 [C]，武汉：湖北教育出版社，2002。

60. 袁行霈编；徐放，韩珊今译；许渊冲英译，新编千家诗 [Z]，北京：中华书局，2006。

61. 袁运，唐宋名诗新译 [C]，海口：南海出版公司，1992。

62. 张智中，李白绝句英译：英汉对照 [Z]，北京：商务印书馆国际有限公司，2021。

63. 张智中，诗意扬州：汉英对照 [Z]，北京：外语教学与研究出版社，2020。

64. 张智中，宋诗绝句150首：今译及英译：汉英对照 [Z]，武汉：武汉大学出版社，2021。

65. 张智中，唐诗绝句英译800首：中英对照 [Z]，武汉：武汉大学出版社，2019。

66. 赵彦春，英韵唐诗百首 [Z]，北京：高等教育出版社，2019。

67. 中国文学出版社编，中国文学：现代诗歌卷（汉英对照）[Z]，北京：中国文学出版社，1998。

68. 朱纯深，古意新声：品赏本（汉英对照）[Z]，武汉：湖北教育出版社，2004。

69. 卓振英，英译宋词集萃：汉英对照 [Z]，上海：上海外语教育出版社，2008。

70. 卓振英、李贵苍，汉诗英译教程 [M]，北京：北京大学出版社，2013。

71. Anne Fremantle, Mao Tse-tung: an Anthology of His Writings — Updated and Expanded to Include a Special Selection of the Poems of Mao, New York, New American Library Inc., 1972.

72. David Hinton. Classical Chinese Poetry: An Anthology[Z]. New York: Farrar, Straus and Giroux, 2008.

73. Owen, Stephen. The Poetry of Du Fu. Boston/Berlin: Walter de Gruyter Inc., 2016.

74. Yang Xianyi & Gladys Yang. Poetry and Prose of the Tang and Song[Z]. Beijing: Chinese Literature Press, 1984.